T0131787

CALL FOR DUTY

JR Reynolds

Order this book online at www.trafford.com
or email orders@trafford.com

Most Trafford titles are also available at major online book retailers.

Printed in the United States of America.

ISBN: 978-1-4269-8989-6 (sc)
ISBN: 978-1-4269-8990-2 (e)

Library of Congress Control Number: 2011914123

Trafford rev. 12/08/2011

 www.trafford.com

North America & international
toll-free: 1 888 232 4444 (USA & Canada)
phone: 250 383 6864 ♦ fax: 812 355 4082

In Memory of

Lt. Col. James Robert Scafe
United States Marine Corps

1932 — 1989

ACKNOWLEDGMENTS

God, for giving me imagination and creativity.

Marian Scafe, who traveled twelve years through school with me and courageously shared the detailed agony of losing her soulmate, a dedicated U.S. Marine exposed to Agent Orange during his tour of duty in Vietnam.

The Las Plumas group, for encouragement and critique: Dave Bartholomew, Cassie Head, Barbara Brown, author Margie Hussey, Sue Meyers, author Don Ulmer, Barbara Boyle, Wayne and Doris Littlefield, Doris my tireless editor, June Goehler, Scott and Jan Stahr, Kathie Arcide, James Fletcher, Lou Chirillo, Skip Buchanan, and author Jim Haskin.

My children, experienced jurors, whose patience, reading and support helped fashion this story. Peggy, Grant, Karlene, Sue, and Grandson Douglas Anthony.

FOREWORD

Joella Simpson, a wife and mother, leads a tranquil domestic life until her modus vivendi is radically altered by two events that challenge her with risk, tragedy, redemption and love.

A moving fable of terse courtroom scenes during her jury duty under a manipulative judicial system, combines with her close involvement in family misfortune concerning her brother-in-law Mark, a Vietnam veteran.

Joella finds she is unqualified and unprepared but forced to accept terms imposed on her that flaw the balance of valued principles in her life.

CHAPTER 1

A long white envelope addressed to my name from the King County Superior Court lay among the mail I retrieved from the console table in the foyer. *Someone is suing me?*

The house is quiet for the first time since early this morning. The children are tucked into their beds. My husband, who operates a big multicolor Heidelberg printing press on second shift, will be home soon. *I know it doesn't concern a moving violation.*

Threading my way through the house, I pick up a dirty sock, an empty water glass, a pop can, a sweater, school papers, depositing all in proper places as I wend my way to the kitchen. *Maybe the State found some money owed me? Maybe I owe them money?*

At the kitchen table, the hub of all family activities, I sit my weary body down. *Maybe something to do with my foster sons?*

I study the envelope once more before tearing it open. A summons to jury duty? *Me? ... The mother of six children, a forty-seven-year-old haggard, bedraggled housewife?... Jury Duty? Out of the question ... they have to be kidding.*

~ ~ ~

May 15, 1972. Monday morning is a gorgeous sun-warmed spring day. It was two weeks ago I received my jury duty summons. I park my car at the Park and Ride and join the long line of commuters boarding one of several express buses into Seattle.

Judging from the number of people lined up at the Park and Ride, I wonder where the news media get their unemployment statistics. Perhaps it's just another piece of propaganda to overshadow real news.

One of the last to climb aboard, I'm confronted with standing room only. Those without a seat, to keep stable balance, clutch one of two overhead rods running down each side of the aisle, the length of the bus.

Being short and unable to reach the above rods, when the bus lurched forward, I grab out wildly for something stable. It isn't necessary; we're so tightly packed, we sway like wheat shafts in the wind.

Entering the freeway, the bus races for town. Envision, if you will, the sensation of riding with a driver manipulating his vehicle during the Indianapolis Raceway on Memorial Day. Without hesitation, he weaves in and out of traffic at breakneck speed.

Once in the big city, we flow out of the buses into downtown Seattle's mainstream. The foot traffic branches out into small streams entering in, out and around buildings, surging forward, ebbing and flowing to designated destinations.

Entering the doors of the King County Courthouse, in the large crowd awaiting elevators, I recognize some as transit passengers from my bus. Am I then to assume everyone of us is reporting for jury duty?

In a tiny room, a line of people ahead of me are showing their jury summonses, handguns, driver's licenses, bribes, drugs, passports, cameras, liquor bottles and visas. The line behind me spills out into the hallway back to the elevators.

A lady behind a thick glass window glances at my summons along with my driver's license picture identification and points to a large gray-painted, warehouse-sized room with three bare walls but for scotch taped or thumbtacked messages, some quite yellow with age. Above us, pipes of assorted descriptions crisscross the ceiling. Two windows on an outside wall face toward Fifth Avenue traffic and surrounding skyscrapers.

A uniformed short-haired lady, void of makeup, instructs us to be seated on hard metal folding chairs until we are summoned to a courtroom.

This same lady welcomes us in her deep-voiced growl, "You are not to leave the building or use the restrooms without permission during court hours. Please make yourselves comfortable."

Scrutinizing the hard metal chairs without padding, I wonder, *How long will we be asked to endure these cold, rigid chairs? This is all the court system can afford with my tax dollars?*

"I'm about to show you a movie describing court procedures," the lady says, "it provides details in answer to any questions you may have."

She further acts out her role of a hostess, inviting us to help ourselves to paper cups, tea bags, instant coffee and cocoa on a table along one wall—all to be mixed with hot water from a machine across the room. Even the fake cream and sugar are packaged. *This is all there is to offer me as a juror, these refugee beverages? Is this the same packaged beverages the lawyers and judges are offered?*

We, the assembly, pace the room or leaf though dog-eared, outdated architecture magazines with stone cave dwelling data and mechanic periodicals for repairing a 1937 truck. Pages of old and new newspapers lay around. Not being familiar with each other, there is little conversing taking place.

In the dreary room with two or three exposed shop-type florescent lights, I didn't have to imagine, I emotionally experienced the sensation of one found guilty and convicted. Only I'm not guilty of any crime and haven't been convicted, but I forfeited my rights the minute I answered my summons for jury duty. I'm forced to serve a sentence for however long the judge orders my jury duty to last or frees me.

A lady in a designer dress sitting next to me wonders aloud, "Who should I show my excuse from duty?"

The elderly gentleman next to her looked up from the paperback claiming his attention to say, "Take it back to the first room where you came in and ask the woman at the window."

Designer Lady returns in a huff. "I was supposed to show it when I came in; now I have to finish the day here." She heaves a sigh of misery, settles back in her chair and stares, along with me, into space.

Twelve o'clock we're excused for lunch but told to report back promptly by one p.m. *For how many more monotonous hours?* I wonder. *I've a day's work waiting for me at home.*

I enter a crowded restaurant and wonder if the kitchen facilities are cleaner than the dingy dining area. But famished after the early two-toast breakfast, I place my order. The dollar bowl of vegetable-beef soup is delicious and being good and hot, I decided it couldn't be contaminated by whatever lay on the other side of the kitchen door. It came accompanied by two cellophane encased soda crackers. Surely they can't be harmful if ingested.

After lunch, for the first time since eight o'clock this morning, events speed up. Names of seventy-five potential jurors are called and they leave the room. Then another twenty for a six panel jury. The rest of us are excused for the day and told, "Report back promptly at eight o'clock tomorrow morning, this same room."

~ ~ ~

Tuesday, day two. I'm informed; only if selected as a juror will I be compensated and receive bus fare. *If I don't serve as a juror, I'm not paid.* Yesterday was an unproductive wasted day of my life. Has the court system no respect for my pursuit of happiness granted in the Constitution? *Jury duty is nothing more than a form of slave labor.*

The prisoner on trial will have a hot meal waiting at the end of the day and without responsibilities can enjoy a good night's rest. The rest of us innocent citizens must return to our home lives after a day in which we accomplish little other than a great loss of precious time.

Today is a repeat of day one excluding the movie. Those not selected for yesterday's jury panel are back with us to await another summons.

We again pace but are friendlier toward one another today. Many complain of the miserable monotonous waiting. Books and up-to-date periodicals appear from pockets and handbags. Otherwise … we pace.

An American citizen blessed with an overactive imagination, I'm here in this large ugly room that has to be patterned, I'm quite certain, after the German concentration camps of the second World War.

A khaki-uniformed man comes into the room around ten a.m. to demand our attention and call names from a list of potential jurors to follow him.

I am one of the fifty who file into a non impressive, wood paneled courtroom without windows. The room contains an American flag, the judge's bench, and two wooden tables with four chairs per table. We, the potential jurors, cluster behind a small partition referred to as the spectator gallery until we advance to the jury box.

A black-robed judge with wild curly hair sits on his throne. I'm not impressed. This judge, to me, is a glorified lawyer. Lawyers are actors who play out roles between each other. They design the language of laws and then interpret the laws in such a way that a layperson is at a loss to understand.

The uniformed man, known as a bailiff, tells us to sit down, then introduces Judge Daly who welcomes us and explains he will be presiding over the trial of Washington State versus Karin Colby. Her charge is second-degree murder.

"The charge is not," the judge tells us, "to be taken as evidence of guilt. It is an accusation, not a declaration. The defendant is presumed innocent until proven otherwise."

Pretty clear since none of us, I believe, were there to witness the murder.

He doesn't ask if we understand; he doesn't ask for questions. It's his show played by his rules as he sees fit to interpret the law.

It's like medicine where a doctor, in his terminology, explains to the patient his diagnosis of their condition. The patient nods his head in agreement and hopes in his ignorance of the doctor's language that he's not in for a brain removal.

My prejudices come from the legal treatment given my folks when after hard work to save a bit of money for a piece of property, the lawyers of a big conglomerate corporation convinced the court not only to lower the property value, but they had it condemned as well so my parents lost their artesian spring property. I witnessed the despair of lost hope and dreams when they were forced to give up their land.

If jury trials are tried by our peers as the legal system dictates, then I would never qualify to pass judgment on an attorney or judge, which is fine by me. I wouldn't want to be involved in their conviction for fear of later retaliation.

I glance to where I think the accused murderer might sit and to my consternation she is already sitting there. A young woman in her late twenties or early thirties. Her act of oblivion and expressionless face gives the impression she's relaxed; her bent elbow rests on the chair arm with chin in cupped hand. Except for her shaved head and orange kimono, she resembles the youthful clerk at my supermarket.

I wonder what she's done. *Is she a mass murderer? One who caused a fatal accident? Beat or killed a child?*

Judge Daly clears his throat noisily, leans forward onto his elbows and focuses on each of us in turn as he conveys a stern lecture on the seriousness and importance of our responsibility as jurors. "I have little patience with people who try to evade their solemn responsibility with trivial excuses."

His no-nonsense attitude put me in mind of when I was a fresh recruit in Civil Air Patrol. My teacher, without raising his soft voice, instructed, "If you listen and pay attention, the life you save may well be your own."

Finished with his rally speech, the judge fumbles with a stack of papers then sizes us up once again. "This case may take time," he warns. "Is this going to cause undue hardship for anyone?"

The courtroom is silent, a few arms lift.

"The first gentleman … there," Judge Daly indicates by pointing then sits back in his chair as he scrutinizes the first man. "Your name, sir?"

"I'm James Hamm, I have a cruise paid for that leaves Sunday night. I'll be glad to postpone my duty for a later date."

Judge Daly frowns. "You are excused."

"And you? Please state your name and hardship," the judge requests of a young woman.

"I'm Pamela Davis, Your Honor. I'm due in another city to take a prepaid exam. I have my receipt and plane tickets to verify the dates."

Judge Daly silently motions for the bailiff to bring the paperwork forward. "Have you served as a juror before, Miss Davis?" He glances through her papers.

"I have, Your Honor, several times."

"You may be excused." Dismissed, she leaves the room.

"State your name and excuse." He points to the next lady.

"I'm Cynthia Bryant. I'm a single parent with three small children I have to pick up from daycare at a certain hour or I get charged extra. I'm the sole caretaker of the boys."

"Holidays ... overtime ... don't you have a plan-B for babysitting, Ma'am?"

"Yes, Judge Daly, but the ten dollars a day I make here doesn't pay the hourly wage I pay daycare."

"Doesn't your union or your employer compensate for your jury duty time?"

"My employer does. Not in wages but in time off from McDonald's," she stammers. "But nothing for my daycare, Your Honor."

The judge again scrutinizes the jurors. "How would you feel," he reprimands, "if you were accused of something and were arrested, but when it came time to pick out ordinary folks like you for jury duty, your friends weren't willing to do it because they all have flimsy excuses? How would you feel?"

Everyone, including me, squirms and shifts in their seats, some cough lightly.

Reluctantly, the judge excused Cynthia Bryant.

A glance at my wristwatch indicates four o'clock. Judge Daly pauses after his little speech and no other hands are raised to be excused.

Court is adjourned for the day with instructions from the judge, "Everyone is to be punctual when court reconvenes tomorrow at eight o'clock in this room." Judge Daly bangs his gavel down to impress us with his authority.

The bailiff calls us to rise while the judge gathers himself together and departs the courtroom for his chambers. *Where is his olive leaf crown and toga*? I wonder, watching him strut from the room.

~ ~ ~

Wednesday, day three, jury selection for the Karin Colby trial. Judge Daly begins by presenting the two lawyers. He introduces Karin's public defender first—Adam Dowd, dressed in a meticulously pressed gray business suit, his hair neatly trimmed. I notice the wide gold band on the ring finger of his left hand. He appears the same age as the accused and his youthful exuberance plainly shows he's anxious to get the jury selection over with and begin the trial.

"Representing the State is the prosecuting attorney, Jack Clemens," Judge Daly states. *For me, it's not difficult to tell from his tone of voice and smile, he and the Assistant District Attorney are friends.* Mr. Clemens is an overweight, reading glasses, mismatched colors tie and shirt man, but otherwise a pleasant, friendly appearing older gentleman.

Judge Daly next explains how the procedure is initiated. "The process is known as the *voir dire,* or *telling the truth.*" In a monotone, he rapidly describes how each of us will answer a series of questions to see if we are fit to be selected as a juror for this case. "In other words, the accused is to be tried by her peers." He reads twelve names from a list before him. As he reads off the names, they rise to take seats in the jury box. Unfortunately, I am not one of them.

But, I ask myself, *who can qualify if they haven't committed a crime or murdered someone. I size up the people around me, none of them appear to qualify.*

The questions are simple: name, profession and marital status. They then state the occupation of their spouse and ages of their children and describe any previous jury duty experience in detail.

One elderly woman, when questioned, said she'd been a victim of a crime. She'd been attacked one night when she was young and still deathly afraid to go out at night alone, even after all these years.

I caught Adam Dowd's glance up at Judge Daly, whose fleeting frown doesn't indicate he is in any way sympathetic. He thanks the woman without further comment and moves to the next juror.

The man said he delivers Sunday papers for The Seattle Times. Judge Daly inquires if he has read about this case.

His answer was, "No, I work two jobs, I don't have time to read a newspaper."

When all twelve had answered the questions put before them, the judge invites Mr. Dowd, the defense attorney to voir dire the jurors. Mr. Dowd concentrates on a yellow legal pad before him, takes a deep breath and from left to right, questions each individual.

I notice he analyzes answers from those who are overly conservative or religious. When he finished, Mr. Clemens, the prosecutor, questioned each one. He challenges any person whose work in any way involves psychology or psychiatry.

The strain from questioning is showing on the jurors. When all the questions are satisfied, Judge Daly invites the prosecutor to begin the next procedure.

I had no idea of this long drawn-out procedure needed to make up a jury panel.

Mr. Clemens indicates a woman, a former schoolteacher, who also has a degree in social work. "Yer Honor, we would like ta thank and excuse Mrs. Hennesey." She is led away without comment from the judge and replaced by the next juror.

The woman answers the questions and states she'd previously been a police dispatcher. Interviewed by the two lawyers, she is promptly dismissed by Mr. Dowd.

One by one, jurors are called to the box, questioned and dismissed until past lunchtime and we're now into the afternoon. One man came through the questioning procedure and is allowed to stay in the jury box.

Among those dismissed this morning is a woman who admitted she reads mysteries and crime stories. She says she has already made up her mind and could not be convinced she might view the case with an open mind. She is excused. The woman who had been mugged when she was young is sent away. A man who witnessed an assault by a patient at a hospital where he worked and had to see a psychologist is excused. A young woman taking a legal assistant course is dismissed.

Judge Daly calls my name. By this time, those of us involved are sick to death of the selection process. I answer the judge's questions though I'm feeling guilty not to have been honest and stated I believe in capital punishment; I'm also prejudice concerning domestic violence and believe in abortion. I decide if I get through the questioning part, I'll stick it out. I'm intrigued by the young woman's ability to murder; this case fascinates me.

Mr. Dowd raises his head from a legal document on which he's been taking notes. He studies me before asking if I know anything about the case from the newspaper, radio or other source.

I answered with an honest, "No."

"Mrs. Simpson, if someone had … let's say a seizure of some type and during the seizure he kills someone with a blow on the head. Do you think that person should be punished?"

I desperately wanted to say, *yes,* but concluded, "I wouldn't … no."

"Why not?" he asked, his intense stare is making me nervous.

"He wouldn't have … that is, I wouldn't think … have control over his actions or movements, would he?"

"You're saying then," Mr. Dowd suggested, "he didn't intend to kill anyone. Is that what you're telling us?"

"Yes … I guess that's how I mean it to be interpreted."

He's upsetting me, I'm not on trial here. I can't tell if I please him with my answers or if I'm being set up to be dismissed. I'm in a sticky situation.

"Good," he nods. Then he glances away to the other jurors before he says, "Let me point out an issue here. The law states that a person who is too sick … mentally sick … to form the intent to kill, cannot be convicted of murder. He or she should be found not guilty by reason of insanity. And/or committed to an institution for treatment and held there until deemed fit to return to society. Do you disagree with this? Do you think this is being too lenient?"

The room is silent. My answers must have satisfied him. He turns the questioning over to the prosecutor, Mr. Clemens, who stands up slowly, frowns at me, then smiles from behind large old-fashioned black-rimmed spectacles. Along with his mismatched tie and shirt, I notice his shoes aren't polished. For such a cranky appearing man, he oozes extreme charm along with his gentle southern drawl.

He chided one man during the interview for giving a contradictory answer to his question concerning occupation. Instead of getting angry, he smiled and stated, "Sir, Ah'm just makin' sure we're talkin' 'bout the same people here. When you go back ta work … now hep me here … will ya'll be writin' for the same newspaper or will ya'll be writin' freelance?"

Southern dialect, to me, is like listening to music—smooth, soft and melodious to the ear.

Mr. Clemens leans against the table, adjusts his face covering eyeglasses and asks if I know anything about or have any impressions about women who have been involved in the Peace Corps.

"I'm not personally acquainted with anyone that has been in the Peace Corps and am not aware of the operation of their organization."

Mr. Clemens seems interested in my education. "When did ya finish yer nurse's trainin' and what was yer specialty?"

"I didn't, sir," I state. "It wasn't going well so I quit and married my fiancé."

"Do ya work in any phase of the medical field now, Miz Simpson?"

"I don't, sir. I'm a full-time wife, mother and foster mother."

"How many foster children ya'll involved with, Miz Simpson?"

I answered, "Two boys, sir."

"Really?" His question catches me off guard. "Isn't it difficult ta raise boys in a normal situation who come from dysfunctional homes? Don't they carry their carpet bags with 'em, so ta speak?"

"Not if you let them know you care about them, love them and pay attention to their good attributes. I find they thrive."

"Forgive me, Miz Simpson, Ah got me a boy needs shaped up; Ah'm tryin' ta hep him bring his grades up. Ya spose there's a chance ... Ah need someone like ya'll who might set his lame feet on the right path. Get the little drummer goin' in the right direction?"

The sound of laughter erupting in the gallery didn't ease my embarrassment. The others must have watched my face flush; I was too nervous to realize the joke. I didn't join in the laughter or even smile.

I'm here out of curiosity that involves Karin's case. *Will I be capable of keeping an open mind as circumstances unfold?*

Mr. Clemens' next question made me pause and in that moment, Mr. Dowd objects, "The question is designed to prejudice the jury." Thankfully, Judge Daly agreed. The prosecutor's question: "Did I think that mental illness excuses a person from any responsibility to society?"

Judge Daly instructed me not to answer.

The prosecutor, without signs of aggravation, looked as if he might have finished questioning me. With his head to one side he asks, "None of yer foster sons have been back before the court with juvenile problems?"

"No sir, not a one."

Mr. Clemens nods and after a moment's pause, he indicates he has no further questions.

For me, I should have felt the release of tension. Less guilty about the deceit of my principles. After all, I'm lenient with my sons. Why not myself? I found my straight-laced upbringing gives me reason to be judgmental towards others. I classify my parents as hypocrites due to their religious belief, but it's not for me to judge them.

The judge orders court dismissal for the day. He orders, "We will convene back in this room tomorrow at eight o'clock promptly." He bangs his gavel to emphasize his clout.

The bailiff orders us to rise while the judge gathers his papers, straightens his robe and departs the bench for his chambers.

He needs a chariot to go with his toga and olive branches, I decide as I race to catch an express bus for home.

Chapter 2

Thursday, day one of the Colby trial. Late for the bus this morning; I'm without a seat again, so stand for the ride into Seattle while I mentally review yesterday's court proceedings.

Today, the trial begins in earnest; Judge Daly proclaimed his satisfaction of the jury panel and one alternative. I'm on the payroll at last.

My life is busy without accepting the added pressure of jury duty. At five a.m. I shut off the alarm and force myself out of bed to care for family demands before I face a day in court and return home at night exhausted.

Today I realize for the first time the reality of a murder trial. I am expected to decide the guilt or innocence of a young woman with whom I'm unacquainted and who lives a totally different lifestyle than mine. It's an uncomfortable sensation when I realize she knows not only my name but private facts of my life given at the jury inquisition, and I know nothing concerning her.

Another thing I find difficult to understand is how we, a group of law-abiding citizens representing different walks of life, can qualify as jurors. The lawyers throw out the undesirables in order to stack their decks, or their jury in this case. Seems a bit unfair, unjust somehow. Of course, the attorneys want a jury they can manipulate.

The corporate attorneys, whose job it was to legally manipulate my folks out of their valuable property, prospered. My folks lost their battle and their dreams.

I should have been more honest and outspoken about my prejudices and opinions concerning my principles. Too late now.

~ ~ ~

Judge Daly, seated at his bench as we sweep into the room, takes time to arrange his robe before he cheerfully acknowledges us.

He begins the day with instructions. "You are not to talk about the case with one another or anyone outside the confines of the courtroom."

The bailiff interrupts the judge who calls for a fifteen minute recess and hastily leaves the room. Mary Alice, a jury member endowed with a lithe graceful body, envy of most women, and I slip out.

We amble down the hall to the restroom. I comment to Mary Alice, "Wonder why none of the other jurors followed us?"

"Maybe they didn't feel the need for a break." She confesses, "I'm not used to sitting for such long periods of time."

After our fifteen minute break, we saunter into the trial room to face an irritated Judge Daly who angrily reprimands us.

"A recess called for the judge does not give jurors the liberty to take a break, leave the room, or do whatever you fancy. The bailiff dismisses you when I say so."

The bailiff quietly whispered, "Apologize to his Honor."

We rise and stammer our act of contrition. I caught myself before I genuflected before him.

Lunchtime. We are instructed, "Return promptly by one o'clock sharp." The bailiff ordered us to rise before the judge departs the room. I have the urge to raise my right arm and shout after him, "Hail, King Daly, our whole morning's been wasted just sitting around doing nothing."

I make my way down the street to a little sandwich shop. A counter circles the room with stools for seating. Customers stand at three tall tables without chairs in the middle of room. I ordered a tuna fish sandwich with a cup of coffee for a buck-fifty.

I'm eating up my ten dollars a day wages. From now on, when I make the kids' lunches, I'll make one for myself. The coffee isn't good but it's superior to that dried powder, bitter substance provided free for jurors.

My sandwich finished, I still have time to shop—window-shop only. I can't afford to purchase anything on my limited jury income.

Just before one o'clock I'm in the elevator surrounded by fellow jurors; we smile at each other but otherwise the lift is silent.

We leap to our feet like well-trained dogs when Judge Daly enters the room. I'm glad we stand. *Can't imagine having to get down on my knees before him. I hope such an idea never occurs to the judge. I'm surprised he hasn't thought of it already.*

Judge Daly smiles and orders us to "sit" … sit down that is. He calls the two attorneys forward and converses quietly out of jury ear range then sends them back to their tables.

Mr. Dowd, Karin Colby's lawyer, doesn't appear he's pleased with the discussion between Judge Daly, himself and Mr. Clemens.

Judge Daly sits forward to begin his explanation of the next phase of the trial. "Since the defendant is pleading not guilty by reason of insanity, the trial therefore is divided into two parts. The first you will decide is the 'guilt phase'—to determine whether or not the defendant is guilty.

"Then we move to the 'sanity phase'—to prove that although she committed the crime, was she insane at the time?"

This seems unusual to me. I might be a simple layperson to the court, but anyone committing murder is insane. Normal people don't go around killing each other, even though tempted at times. Something inherent restrains us from doing harm. *Why aren't the two phases tried simultaneously? I don't understand why the court has to make issues so difficult and time consuming.*

~ ~ ~

The prosecutor, Mr. Clemens, gives his opening argument first. No better dressed than the day before, he relates to us in his southern drawl how the defendant, Karin Colby, bored and unsatisfied with campus life, dropped out of college, drifted to California and joined the Peace Corps for excitement.

"After a few months, Miss Colby became disenchanted with the Peace Corps and returned ta Washington, her home state, ta search for a church ta satisfy her blossomin' interest in religion.

"One day Miss Colby gets irritated with an older gentleman—mid-sixties fella. Miss Colby here, the defendant, gets belligerent and 'stead of showin' good sense un walkin' away, she assaults this man. Miz Colby grabs a heavy wooden stick outta the man's hands un proceeds ta club him over the head and shoulders till the poor fella, fightin' for his life un clearly no match for the young woman, is knocked ta the floor."

Mr. Clemens pauses before our jury box. "We have bystanders who witnessed the assault. That older gentleman ... Mr. Nishimura died immediately followin' the trauma brought about by blows ta the head that crushed Mr. Nishimura's skull."

As Mr. Clemens describes the crime, I silently assess young Karin, her size, her youth and physical condition. *Not hard to believe she might inflict lethal blows that would produce the skull battering Mr. Clemens describes.*

Did Karin Colby learn how to attack from Peace Corps training in self-defense? Young people can be brainwashed to the point they lose respect for human life. Has she no empathy for one less fortunate than herself? No respect for senior citizens?

A stir from the back of the room. We turn to see a group of Orientals surrounding an elderly man and woman. I gather the young men and women consoling the older folks are members of the murdered victim's family.

Mr. Clemens concludes as he points at the defendant and stares straight at her ... "Miss Karin Colby here ... in fine physical condition ... intentionally killed Mr. Nishimura in order ta demonstrate her jealous insensitivity against a man.

"If Miz Colby," the prosecutor's voice lowers to a soft drawl to emphasize his statement, "wasn't so full of self-pity, selfishness and insecurity, she'd see people respect and commend her for wantin' ta promote peace. All the woman had ta do is choose a peaceful path advocated by other young women of her generation.

"When you've heard all the evidence, Ah believe ya'll will find ya have no other choice but ta find the defendant guilty." Mr. Clemens waddles slowly back to his chair.

After a brief pause, Judge Daly orders the defense Mr. Dowd to make his opening statement. The judge has to prod him. It's obvious Mr. Dowd is still harboring a grudge.

Mr. Dowd rises and slowly walks over to face us. "Ladies and gentlemen of the jury. At this time, I'm forbidden to introduce evidence of mental illness during the *guilt phase* of the trial. You, the jury, therefore are forced to go through the process of declaring Karin Colby guilty of murder before I have a chance to properly defend her. My greatest hope is that when this part of the trial is over, you will be open-minded to hear evidence of insanity. Thank you."

Heads turn to watch Judge Daly's reaction. His lifted eyebrow signaled he was about to rebuke Mr. Dowd, but the eyebrow settled back in place. The prosecutor Mr. Clemens chuckled quietly.

As I stated in the beginning, the judge and two lawyers are in competition and may the most convincing player win. These men are friends outside of court; they probably play golf together, even attend family functions. They may also owe each other a favor. What of the accused? May God have mercy on Karin. We may never hear the story from her lips.

Before taking an afternoon break, we are again instructed not to discuss any of the proceedings until deliberations start.

Mike, one of the jurors, a short, beefy squat man, mutters loud enough for everyone around him to hear, "Until the deliberations start? What the hell does that mean?" I smile and quickly turn away from him.

Why do I assume things will be better explained as we continue along? What is the procedure of a trial? I suppose, in view that teachers in public schools are busy with overloaded classrooms and heavy teaching obligations, they don't have time to teach a course on jury proceedings or legal jargon. Schools don't teach how to balance a checkbook, much less teach a class on handling family situations.

People who've previously served as jurors, I don't recall them ever explaining procedures or court terminology. Why isn't this part of our education? How does the average juror know what to expect? So we citizens, eligible for jury duty, go into it blindly. Mike is a fine example.

I pretend to concentrate on the view of the street below, hoping to discourage anyone, especially Mike, from breaking my meditation, but he saunters over beside me.

He asks, "You a sports fan?"

I answer, "I'm not."

He's not to be discouraged. "Last night the Rainiers suffered an embarrassing defeat," he complains. "Course the other team's a shitty team, but it doesn't make sense. A great team plays a crappy team, and somehow it rubs off and the crappy team makes the good team play crappy. Know what I mean?"

He adjusts his pants. Earlier, I noticed his protruding beer belly; he probably has skinny legs and definitely no behind. At least he isn't discussing the trial.

One of the women jurors standing close by overhears his conversation and drifts our way.

"Why don't they pipe in music? It would give us a lift." Her even white teeth combine with a broad grin to give her the Hollywood smile. When neither Mike or I comment, she excuses herself to have a cigarette.

After our return to court and honoring Judge Daly, the State's first witness is called ... a tall, lanky man wearing an orange kimono, a replica of Karin Colby's. Mr. Earl Bender's head is not a shiny bald but has a freshly shaved appearance.

I envision him years earlier as a well-coordinated young athlete. One of those strikingly handsome young men of classic Greek or Italian stud origin.

Today he still balances on the balls of his feet, elbows out, his bowed legs outlined in his kimono. Probably lumpy cramped leg muscles tightly squeezed against other muscles. I estimate his weight to be one-fifty but probably truer to one-forty. *Certainly not a football halfback, if he ever was one.*

Mr. Bender, passing the jury box on the way to the witness stand, chooses to ignore us but glares at the defendant who nods; a hint of a smile crosses her face.

Mr. Bender, after taking the oath, is invited by the bailiff to sit down. He poses in a rigid unnatural erect position, his hands folded in his lap.

Something tells me he's been in some kind of training to assume such upright posture.

Mr. Clemens approaches halfway between the jurors and the witness stand. He nonchalantly gazes about the courtroom.

I wonder ... *Is his intent to express a relaxed atmosphere?*

Mr. Clemens then instructs Mr. Bender to introduce himself.

"I'm a senior resident monk of the Kirkland Zen Foundation church."

This explains his shaved head.

Mr. Clemens then instructs him to describe the day of the murder.

"Our church members were conducting a meditation practice during the winter retreat." Mr. Bender describes, "The tradition requires we hold to a rigorous daily schedule of rising at four o'clock in the morning, performing in front of a Buddha image then prostrating while chanting in Japanese. Our next practice is to sit absolutely still for up to sixteen hours in meditation.

"We, who are in charge, send the students off to bed at eleven o'clock at night. But many of them," Mr. Bender informs us, "only pretend to follow our orders. In their determination to show their devotion, they sneak back down to the meditation hall and continue their meditation. I, myself, have caught them doing this.

"The purpose of the meditation," he details, "is to find a solution to an irrational problem that our Zen Master privately assigns each student. The student can solve the problem only if they have the *transformational insight*, known as *enlightenment*."

Mr. Bender continues, "On our fourth day, in the morning, Karin began showing difficulties with her meditation. She was restless and nervous. We all thought she was trying to transcend into deep concentration. It annoyed us but no one was concerned about her.

"I need to explain … talking is forbidden during the entire retreat. So after a lunch, observed in complete silence, the students began hour long periods of meditation."

I wonder, as must have all of the jurors, *How can anyone actually manage to sit cross-legged for so many hours? I've seen Eastern meditation done without losing concentration. How do they keep some abstract object from defusing their focused meditation?*

If this practice is done for sixteen or more hours a day, does it produce a euphoric elation or are the results like a penance with repetitive repeats of a phrase?

Suddenly it occurred to me. *People do this all the time—dancers, musicians, actors. There are jobs in the workforce that require torturous, unbearable hours spent in repetitive work.*

Mr. Bender continues, "Sometime after the first hour of meditation, we heard Karin softly weeping, but she seemed in control so I thought she was all right.

"Then during the second hour," Mr. Bender said, "Karin still appeared okay and in control, but during our walking exercise, we … that is I … noticed she walked with a stagger, like she didn't have good balance. During a walking period, we stretch and bend to exercise our muscles. But when Karin walked … her steps were … were like she … she walked with a strange limp to her step.

"We returned to our lotus positions. Then it began … her strange behavior. With a smile she began to mumble. The instructor signaled for her to be quiet and that's when she leaped up and began chanting out loud—"

Mr. Clemens interrupts him. "Would ya mind tellin' the court… exactly what she said?"

"She said … yes, I remember exactly what she said … 'I've the answer to the problem I've been given to solve. I'm a Buddha … I'm a Buddha, I don't deserve this,' she yelled."

The jury, along with Mr. Bender, glances over at the defendant, who nodded her head slowly in agreement with what Mr. Bender described.

"So … then Mr. Nishimura," the monk continued, "demands of Karin, 'You've shown disrespect as a Buddha nun. I think you better leave the room.'"

Mr. Bender stayed silent until urged by Mr. Clemens, "And then, sir …ya mind tellin' the court here what happened next?"

We leaned forward to hear Mr. Bender describe the details.

"Yes, well … Karin was quiet a moment, then she grabbed the heavy stick Mr. Nishimura carried … she grabbed it out of his hand … she struck Mr. Nishimura.

"She … she hit Mr. Nishimura on the head, in the face and on his shoulders … she rained blow after blow to Mr. Nishimura time and time again. We were paralyzed with shock … it was unbelievable … unreal to watch … Karin kept striking him, even after Mr. Nishimura fell and the blood … so much blood … blood spattered. I could see

Mr. Nishimura's skull was broken, it was open … caved in … there was blood everywhere."

The jurors witness Mr. Bender close his eyes, his hands ball into tight fists in his lap, otherwise his posture never wavers.

We, the jurors, strained to hear Mr. Bender.

"You had to know him … Mr. Nishimura … he was wonderful."

We observe, for the first time, Mr. Bender fight to keep his composure.

"Mr. Nishimura was so gifted," Mr. Bender's voice barely audible, "an inspiration to us all … he touched the lives of so many people."

Loud sobbing came from the back of the room behind the attorneys where the victim's elderly sister gave into anguish.

I turn to see two young women desperately trying to comfort her. The woman's husband or perhaps brother, sat rigid, staring straight ahead. Tears run down his face, but he refrains from wiping them away.

My concept at hearing Mr. Bender's account was one of utter contempt for Karin. Glancing over at her, I caught an almost euphoric smile on her face. *How could she? She killed a man … a mid-sixties man … she had to be insane to have carried out such a deplorable act. I, a member of the jury, am asked by the judge to decide her guilt, not her sanity. How is this possible? The woman is guilty; Mr. Bender just explained Karin's insane action.*

I glance around to my fellow jurors. Some shift nervously, others sit expressionless and quiet.

We watch the witness pull himself together before Mr. Clemens questions him.

"Do ya need a drink of water, Mr. Bender? Ah apologize, Ah know this hasta be difficult but would ya mind tellin' us what happened next?"

"No water, thank you." Mr. Bender is immediately in control and continues to describe what he witnessed.

"After Karin struck Mr. Nishimura eight or maybe ten times, I rushed to tackle Karin to the floor. Other members came to help me and someone called the police."

Mr. Clemens turns abruptly, pointing to the clerk. "Please bring in exhibit number one."

The clerk returns with a heavy wooden stick, covered with dark stains.

Mr. Clemens gingerly lifts the exhibit. "Is this the oak stick Karin Colby used ta kill Mr. Nishimura?"

"Yes."

Mr. Clemens carries the exhibit over and insists, "Ah want each of ya ta hold this ta get a sense of how heavy it is."

I feel a queasiness rise up from my stomach when it's my turn to touch and handle an object that killed a man. The sensation is upsetting to say the least.

After the heavy stick is returned to the clerk, Mr. Clemens resumed his examination of the witness.

"Mr. Bender, after ya tackled Karin ta the floor, what was she like … like did she put up a struggle? Tell the court … did she say anything to ya? Tell us somethin' about what took place next."

"She told me she'd been *enlightened*. She realized her koan, said she was a *bhikkhuni (Buddhist nun)*."

I caught the rapid exchange of expressions between Mr. Bender and Karin. The witness frowns with disgust; the defendant appears to be listening attentively.

The defendant's chair scraped on the tile floor as she moved it. I thought she was going to stand up and say something. But Mr. Dowd put his hand on Karin's wrist and whispered something to her in time to prevent a disturbance. A detached, vague expression crossed Karin's face.

I couldn't help but wonder if her public defender was actually encouraging her to appear insane.

I glanced at my watch, nearly four o'clock. Express buses run fifteen minutes apart up until six p.m. I have a day's work ahead of me, kids to collect from soccer practice and music lessons. Dinner to get on the table, clothes to wash. I feel like a race horse … ready to fly … the minute I step off the bus.

Judge Daly announces that the first cross-examination of the trial, by the prosecuting attorney has been satisfied and we will resume with Mr. Dowd's defense tomorrow.

~ ~ ~

Washington State Superior Court does not begin new cases on Friday. Jurors already serving on cases must report every day until the case is settled and are excused only for weekends or holidays. Other potential jurors return Monday morning and wait to be called for a case or until excused from further reporting. Unfortunately, I must report tomorrow.

On the bus ride home, I discover I'm exhausted from another stressful day. My thoughts glow like live coals. My mind refuses to set aside details of Karin Colby's attack on Mr. Nishimura.

The extreme, drastic shift from court to domestic duties finds me literally drained, worn out as I step off the bus, head for my car and home.

CHAPTER 3

Friday, the second day of the trial, I'm weighed down by problems at home. How long will my children accept the changes made to their daily living? They understand it's not forever but for how long will their lives be disrupted? Besides, school will soon be out and then what? Plans for our summer have been set aside with this trial disturbing our lives.

I face the day bothered with the question of Karin Colby's sanity for the murder of a mid-sixties gentleman. There's no question that the act was insane, but what if it were deliberate? At the beginning of this trial, I questioned my opinion on recognizing a person's sanity. I am still at a loss for an answer.

The fine line between sanity and insanity has always been considered a debatable issue. Rages of temper are sins according to my religion … explained in the ten commandments as "Thou shall not kill." We are out of control during such moments … totally insane and must be held accountable for our choice of action.

The first recorded murder in history comes from the Bible. God, seeing that Adam and Eve broke his commandment by eating an apple from the tree of knowledge, He demanded they slaughter their beloved animals to cover their nakedness and use the blood as sacrifice, atonement for their wickedness.

Adam and Eve had two sons. Cain, the first born, raised sheep; Abel, his kid brother, chose to be a gardener.

Scripture reads: 'Little brother Abel killed his brother Cain out of jealousy when God accepted Cain's sacrifice of animals but rendered Abel's plants unacceptable.'

Abel's penance for the murder of his brother Cain was to wander the rest of his days on earth. Any ground on which he tried to sow seed would always be barren; however, God spared his life.

Washington State's death penalty corresponds with the Eighth Amendment to the United States Constitution, which acknowledges a death penalty but forbids 'cruel and unusual' punishment. And interestingly cites nothing concerning insanity.

~ ~ ~

Inside the courtroom, we seat ourselves in the same chairs we chose when first sequestered as jurors. The day begins with our hearing the cross-examination of the witness by the defense attorney, whose determination is to let us know of the bizarre behavior carried on at Zen retreats.

Mr. Dowd addresses the monk, who is returned to the witness stand. "Mr. Bender," he begins, "I'd like to start by having you describe Mr. Nishimura's oak stick. Could you tell us something about it?"

Mr. Bender appears a bit nervous, but his rigid posture remains straight and his hands placed in his lap are relaxed. He answers, "The stick referred to is a Kyosaku, a wooden stick shaped like a paddle used by all Zen teachers."

Mr. Dowd shows interest with a nod and utters a low "humm" as Mr. Bender describes the heavy wooden stick. Mr. Dowd then turns from leaning on the railing by Mr. Bender, to capture the jury's attention. "Mr. Bender, tell us … how is it used?"

"Sometimes Zen teachers use it to … to … well, to prod. Say a student gets drowsy and you can tell their mind is wandering … then—"

"Mr. Bender," Mr. Dowd interrupts the monk, "tell us, how is it used?" Again, Mr. Dowd doesn't give Mr. Bender time to answer. "Isn't it true, Mr. Bender, the teacher strikes … hits you with it?"

Mr. Bender fidgets in his chair. "Sure, across the back, but he doesn't do it without reason … it's a gesture of kindness … it's only meant to help us."

"Kindness?" Mr. Dowd's voice conveys sarcasm. "Some kindness. How hard does he strike with the stick?"

"Oh, not hard … more like a slap. Students look forward to it … especially if their back is tired from sitting for a long time."

"Had Mr. Nishimura ever hit Karin with the stick in question?"

"Well, of course," the monk is obviously nervous, "he uses it on all the students."

"Tell us, Mr. Bender," Mr. Dowd raises his voice, "didn't he use it on Karin just before Karin went hysterical that afternoon?"

"Yes, but not right before … it was several … well … several minutes prior to the attack."

Mr. Dowd nods, his facial expression shows skepticism. He's not convinced. I can tell by his next statement. "Mr. Bender, you didn't give us these details in your earlier testimony."

"But, I did," the monk's relaxed manner gives way to agitation, "I said Mr. Nishimura signaled Karin to quiet down. A strike with the Kyosaku is a signal used on everyone. Students of Zen know about it and its use, it didn't originate out of thin air, sir … Mr. Dowd."

"So," Mr. Dowd said, "Mr. Nishimura signaled her, meaning he struck her with the oak stick to quiet her down. Then a few minutes later, according to your testimony, Karin suddenly began screaming that she's a Buddha and has the answer to her koan."

A silence fills the courtroom before Mr. Dowd inquires, "Did it occur to you … any of you … at any point … that maybe Karin, Miss Colby, wasn't all right?"

The monk shakes his head. "It might occur to you that way, but crying and laughing happens to students during these retreats, but Karin's hallucinating happened a lot. She acts strangely, but not so that any of us could have been aware she would do something like what she did."

"Mr. Bender," the lawyer asks with a look of disbelief, "are you not aware that inappropriate laughing, crying and hallucinating also happens during psychotic occurrences?"

The witness wipes his hands along his thighs. "I'm no expert on that, no."

We watch him continue stroking his palms, then the backs of his hands along the sides of his kimono.

"I'm aware of that, Mr. Bender," Mr. Dowd says, "but … all right … let's move on to solving the puzzle, then. Can you tell us anything about the koan Mr. Nishimura assigned Karin?"

"It's difficult to explain the context of this. You see … Zen koans aren't logical."

We, the jury, watch Mr. Bender's face turn beet red. "Sometimes they seem … well … it's like they don't make sense. They sound strange. Their purpose is to make you understand your reasoning limitations."

Mr. Dowd nods but remains silent. The witness eventually realizes he isn't free of guilt. He places a hand to his mouth covering a nervous cough before continuing. "The koan Karin was given is very well known. It's been used for thousands and thousands of years and goes like this …" Mr. Bender restlessly fidgets before he says, "If you meet a Buddha in the road and he stands in your way …" Mr. Bender's voice is barely audible, "you kill him."

Mr. Dowd glances over to see if we share his puzzlement, his confusion.

"Mr. Bender, that does sound bizarre; can you give us the correct interpretation of Mr. Nishimura's advice to 'Kill the Buddha in the road.'?"

"Oh, no, I haven't passed my koan yet."

"Then, Mr. Bender, are we to assume that according to Zen philosophy, a Zen master is considered a living Buddha?"

Mr. Bender nods his head rapidly. "Yes, that is correct … this is true."

I look to catch Mr. Dowd's expression, but he faces away with his hands clasped behind his back; he nods and begins reviewing the information aloud.

"Mr. Bender, in your testimony, you said Mr. Nishimura was a living Buddha. Is this not true? Is this correct?"

"Yes, sir, this is true … this is correct."

"So," Mr. Dowd reiterates, "when Karin's shouting began, it was because she knew the answer to the puzzle? Mr. Nishimura ordered her to show, to demonstrate she knew what she was talking about? Is this correct?"

"Yes."

"Interesting." Mr. Dowd with a hint of a smile turns to the jurors then slowly returns to his table next to the defendant.

There was a dramatic pause in the interrogation. Mr. Dowd, before sitting down, looked up at Judge Daly. "The defense has no further questions, Your Honor."

Before the close of court, I notice the looks between the Buddha monk and Karin Colby. Karin, who is facing a charge of murder, smiles and appears more sane than her Buddha brother who displayed a look of rage at the Buddha nun.

~ ~ ~

Saturday morning I rise to face a busy weekend. I appreciate my friends I encounter who are aware I'm serving on jury duty and show respectful silence concerning the case.

I'm also appreciative they take time to drop off delectable, prepared dishes to ease my load and help by including my children with theirs to attend games and school functions.

They traded stories of their experiences while serving jury duty. Some of the episodes were humorous, others tragic. It didn't really amaze me when I suggested jury duty as a permanent position that the response was unfavorable.

Someone said, "It was my civic obligation and not over too soon."

I promised my curious husband if he insists on questioning my jury duty, I'm moving out to the couch. I understand his interest but his, "What's it like and is the case interesting?" only brings more questions on a subject I'm pledged to avoid.

I'm still plagued with making a decision concerning another person's life. The people around me … are we all sane? Who is qualified to say? Are there definite guidelines that define sanity and are we educated enough to identify them?

Is Karin Colby guilty of murder or insane? Mr. Clemens, the prosecuting attorney advises Karin is guilty. Karin did brutally kill a man … a mid-sixties gentleman.

But someone insane isn't mentally in control of their mind. Is insanity on the wrong side of the law?

CHAPTER 4

Monday morning the trial's third day. I awake to a definite change in the weather. Sometime during the night a band of clouds rolled in under the cover of darkness, waiting impatiently to advance along with the day as they hang suspended, dark and threatening above the city.

I'm reluctant to abandon my bed at such an early hour. The weekend, like a sleek cat on silent paws, came and disappeared without leaving tracks, while I washed, cleaned, prepared food for the week, attended church, and even attended the kids' soccer games. I fell into bed totally exhausted each night; this is not my idea of what life is about.

I run for the express bus in a misty drizzle so common in this part of the country. Today on the ride into Seattle I'm fortunate to bag a seat.

Following courtroom formalities, we seat ourselves and Judge Daly calls a State witness—the young police officer who first arrived at the scene and took Karin Colby into custody. The officer, a very young man, doesn't smile. He appears unaware of us, the jury, and answers the attorneys with clipped precision answers, always including, *sir*.

In spite of his formal attempt to make his testimony fact and nothing more, he let us know he thinks Karin Colby is a self-absorbed abnormal woman that knew exactly what she was doing when she was arrested.

The prosecutor inquired, "Did Miss Colby appear in control of herself when ya arrested her?"

"Yes, sir, the suspect did not resist arrest; she wasn't agitated and was in complete control."

"And, sir, after ya read her her rights, did she speak ta ya at all?"

"Yes, sir, the suspect talked quite a bit."

"Would ya mind tellin' the court what she talked about?"

"The suspect spoke about her viewpoint … her philosophy I believe she called it. It made little sense to me, just a lot of gibberish nonsense. She said something about illusions but didn't explain herself. She was too busy complaining the handcuffs were cutting off her circulation and demanding I adjust them. Also, sir, on the way to the station she told me to avoid using the freeway because a congestion would delay us."

"And was she right, Officer?"

The officer nervously stirred. "Yes, sir, we were delayed for a time."

I watch the policeman's reaction, he is obviously embarrassed having to agree with the prosecutor, that the suspect, especially a woman, was correct.

Mr. Clemens addresses the bench, "No further questions, Yer Honor."

Judge Daly excuses the police officer after his questioning is satisfied and Mr. Dowd has no questions.

We are excused for a fifteen minute break. I couldn't wait to ask Mary Alice, my juror compatriot, which counterpart she thinks our heroic judge resembles … Caligula, Nero, or Brutus?

I knew she'd be amused. She comments that to her, Judge Daly resembles a huge bird. "He spreads out those flowing sleeves of his robe like they're wings."

I laughed then and I laugh now to picture this big black bird residing over his roost with a little crown of olive leaves atop his bushy head and drooping over one eye. His shiny, black, hawk-like eyes never missing a detail. If only we were in a marble coliseum to complete this scene.

"A bird ... a big black bird with the head of Brutus," she giggles. "Brutus, to me, is dignified, regal, and pompous."

Returned to our jury seats, we are introduced to the next State witness, a homicide detective who interviewed Karin Colby after her arrest. This man is friendlier than the officer before him had been. The detective, a black man with a thin, trim mustache, speaks without the military precision terminology used by the previous officer.

I observe him glance in the defendant's direction several times without any outward sign of hostility or apparent malevolence.

"Mr. White," Mr. Clemens inquires, "did Miss Colby make a confession ta ya?"

Mr. White scoots back in his seat, folds one leg over the other and answers, "Yes, she did."

"Ya'll read her the Miranda rights, did ya?"

"Yes."

"And would ya mind tellin' us what it was she said?"

"She was very cooperative and acknowledged immediately that she'd killed a man. When I questioned her further, she said she didn't feel any remorse. She said the killing was something that we wouldn't understand—that only Buddha people know about these things. She said it is common knowledge between Zen students. She didn't feel there was much point in going into detail when it was something I wouldn't understand anyway.

"She feels the victim, the Oriental fellow ... Mr. Nishimura, would have understood the killing ... that only Zen members can understand this rationale."

"Did Miss Colby say what Mr. Nishimura's doctrine was? His doctrine bein' the same as his philosophy, Ah take it?"

"Well, she tried to explain it to me," Mr. White chuckled, "but her explanation went right over my head. Me not being a Zen and all. It's written in my report ... my report is better than me relying on my memory.

"Miss Colby gave me to think," the detective continued, "this whole Zen thing is about confidence. That if a person is to have complete confidence in themselves, anything they do must be perfect. While I agree this sounds great ... cults make things work this way ... that is ... until you see what they lead up to and how people … how they make people do things that aren't normal."

Mr. Clemens nods slowly before addressing Judge Daly. "That'll be all, Yer Honor." We watch Mr. Clemens shuffle back to his table.

Judge Daly thanks the witness, excuses him after Mr. Dowd has no questions at this time, and at the same time dismisses us for lunch after we are reminded we swore an oath of secrecy concerning the trial.

I find this request difficult. It's a current event for us jurors, it's the highlight of our lives at the moment.

Mary Alice and I decide to stay indoors out of the rain. In the hall, outside the courtroom, benches and a few chairs line the wall. These are for witnesses waiting to be called into the courtroom when they are needed.

We tote a couple chairs to a secluded spot but not before Mike discovers us and isn't about to remain alone.

Creating unnecessary noise, he drags a chair across the floor and positions it near Mary Alice—so willowy and graceful. Attributes I admire—the exact opposite of me. Then he loudly comments, "This whole damn thing is crazy. Like one of them detective shows my kids watch on TV. I'm not much on crime movies, myself, they're all alike."

I see he's without lunch and offer him half of my tuna sandwich, which he declines. "An apple, then?" I suggest.

"Nah," he says, "I don't work up an appetite when I'm not doing physical work. I sure get a kick out of how them witnesses tell their side of the story."

Mary Alice and I hastily trade looks. We attempt to quiet him. We heard him suppress his amusement a couple of times while the testimonies were being heard.

He isn't to be silenced, that's for sure.

"The idea that a bald lady hit another baldy with a club is kinda stupid, I think … well, don't you think so?" He waits for us to agree.

"Grown folks and they call 'emselves priests and nuns. Ha!"

Mary Alice corrects him. "Mike, I think they're called monks." Then she quickly asks, "I forgot, Mike … what is it you do for a living?"

"I work down at Todd Shipyards, a crane-operator."

At last we wean him away from the trial. Mary Alice and I spend the rest of the lunch hour initiating conversations away from any mention of court issues.

We resume our seats for the afternoon testimonies. Judge Daly invites the defense to call their witness.

Mr. Dowd declines saying, "My witness for the defense has nothing to say if they aren't allowed to discuss Miss Colby's mental condition, Your Honor."

I watch Judge Daly lift his dramatic eyebrow and shrug. "If you and Mr. Clemens are through with the witnesses, then I believe we're ready to hear your closing arguments, gentlemen."

I'm not educated enough to pass judgment on the position of the public defender. However, I assume, these men entertain some degree of competence to represent their client, especially a murder trial such as this. Mr. Dowd appears to have little interest in representing his client.

Mr. Clemens leads off. He approaches us in his slow mannered waddle and reviews the testimonies in his relaxed southern drawl. "The witnesses describe the crime in irrefutable testimony, this then leaves no room for doubt that the defendant, Miss Karin Colby, *intentionally* killed Mr. Nishimura."

I'm shocked, as I'm sure the rest of the jurors are, when Mr. Dowd declines to make a closing argument in behalf of his client.

Judge Daly announces the evidence part of the trial is now over. He then rattles off some brief instructions about the law, how it's written, and how we are to apply it to the evidence and arrive at a verdict.

"Let me remind you," he pauses momentarily, "a crime of second-degree murder requires that it be an intentional killing … not an accident … it does not require Miss Colby to have planned or thought about the crime beforehand. Even if the killing was entirely impulsive, it still counts as murder if the defendant possessed the intent to kill when she swung the heavy wooden paddle."

Why else would she have swung the wooden stick repeatedly, Judge Daly, but to murder the Zen master? We must decide her guilt? And why isn't Karin allowed to tell her version?

The bailiff requests we rise and follow him as he leads us behind Judge Daly's podium and into the deliberating room furnished with a long highly polished oak table and thirteen chairs. Mary Alice and I grab chairs next to each other near the middle of the table. The last person in the room takes the one remaining chair, which everyone is avoiding because of its location at the head of the table.

The bailiff instructs us, "The first thing you do is elect a foreman or speaker to represent the jury. Anyone, except the alternative juror, can be a foreman."

Mr. Donaldson, the last person to enter the room, was not the alternative juror. By a unanimous vote, Mr. Donaldson becomes the foreman.

The heavyset man with a disciplined manner about him, doesn't seem to mind his newly acquired foreman position.

"Okay, this parts over and we're here," he states. "Let's move forward.

"I served on a previous jury before this," Mr. Donaldson tells us. "What we did was, we cast a secret ballot first. Then reviewed the evidence as a group before voting a second time. If you approve of my suggestion, then let's hand out slips of paper and write either 'guilty' or 'not guilty' on them. Oh, and the alternative juror is not allowed to vote, only when he or she assumes the rights of a juror can they vote."

"No … wait a second," a housewife, Mrs. Judson, raises her hand. "What if a juror … what if someone is undecided … what do they do … what should they write?"

Oh, no, I thought. *There's one in every crowd isn't there?* I glance at Mary Alice, and from her frown, I know she shares my opinion.

"That's a good question," Mr. Donaldson replies. "Then you will need to write undecided … that's my suggestion."

I feel I have little choice, so I write 'guilty.' I can't help wondering if the second half of the trial is going to be more complicated.

The folded once over papers are handed down to Mr. Donaldson. We mentally count as he opens the folded papers and lays them in a pile. That's it … all but one.

Looking up at us, he smiles. "Eleven guilty, one undecided."

An exasperated Mrs. Judson fumes. "Well, so much for the secret ballot."

"Don't worry about it, Mrs. Judson. Don't let this procedure upset you."

Mrs. Judson wasn't to be placated. "I don't see the direction we're headed for in here." We hear the anxiety in her voice. "I mean … I heard the same evidence as the rest of you and it's not obvious to me that everything is out in the open here, as the vote seems to indicate."

A silence follows. I'm thinking, *Mrs. Judson is having difficulty thinking clearly or is it in expressing herself. Yet, she's right, I feel too, that I'm only hearing part of the story.*

Mr. Donaldson exhibits responsibility as our foreman. "Mrs. Judson," he patiently responds, "What would you have us do? Do you want us to go over the evidence? What parts are giving you problems?"

Mrs. Judson's attitude changes dramatically from whiner to combative. "Well," she huffs, "I'm feeling pressured for one thing. I feel like I'm being put on the witness stand. I'm uncomfortable and I don't appreciate being cornered."

I glance around to see jury members contemplating fingernails, staring around the room, or simply concentrating on the table.

The silence continues until Mrs. Judson speaks again. "I haven't said Miz Colby isn't guilty. I just don't think she's been *proven* guilty. What I mean to say is … that man … the leader of their cult … the Japanese man Miss Colby killed … well, didn't one of the witnesses say the man who was killed …that he knew what was coming?"

Breathlessly she continued. "Now, you take our President Roosevelt. He was a monster, he got away with doing evil things—was he treated like a murderer? And what about that My Lai massacre where all those people were slaughtered. Who gave the orders to do that vile thing? William Calley or was it General Westmoreland? These men … they are the evil ones. Didn't some monk centuries ago write and give the order to kill? How can we find Miz Colby guilty? And another thing, we haven't even heard Miss … Karin's side of the story."

To the rest of us, including myself, Mrs. Judson's comparisons aren't out of line. No one gave her an argument, no one wants to tackle this lady.

Mrs. Judson, thoroughly exasperated, blurts out, "You are all so sure she's guilty, aren't you?" She glares at each one of us. "Then I guess I must be missing something. So if you insist she's guilty, that's fine … go ahead … whatever … if you say so … then she's guilty … she's guilty… Okay? Mark me down, Mr. Donaldson, she's guilty."

The room is silent, no one encourages Mrs. Judson to stand by her convictions. We accept her surrender.

"Good … then it's unanimous?" Mr. Donaldson asks. We nod our approval. "Then our vote is confirmed."

My thoughts are, *Yes, we better hightail it back into the courtroom before Mrs. Judson entertains second thoughts.* We return to our jury box seats.

I feel the defendant closely monitors each of us. When she focuses on me, I start to look away but catch myself. *Why not look her in the face?* I return her stare, feeling strange, as I did when I held the murder weapon. Her face reveals nothing, she's utterly relaxed, she stares at me out of curiosity. We hold our stare for a few seconds before she breaks contact and diverts her stare to someone else.

I catch her searching Mary Alice's face and see them exchange smiles. She doesn't even know how we voted. She appears so innocent, so naive.

A lamb being led to slaughter? But I had no choice, Karin … all the evidence points to guilty in this first phase of your trial.

CHAPTER 5

I rush for home to prepare dinner before I pick up the kids from soccer practice and music lessons.

The tater-tots and fish sticks are ready for the oven as soon as I return from collecting the family. Just as I grab my purse and cars keys, the phone rings. I debate whether to answer or just keep going. For some reason, I pick up the receiver.

My little sister Paula's voice surprises me at this hour. She works the afternoon shift as a nurse's aide at a nursing home in Fife.

Life is difficult for Paula with two little ones and a troubled husband at home. Though the Pentagon refuses to admit the problem, Mark's been exposed to Agent Orange, a deadly weed killer used by the Marine Corps during his Vietnam tour of duty in 1968. He's now unable to hold down full-time employment with his problems that keep him fatigued with headaches and muscle weakness. He's not the same man who went to war.

I immediately detect something wrong from the sound of her voice.

I see by the kitchen clock I'm running late. In a controlled voice I answer, "Hi, Sis."

"Something terrible has happened." Sobs muffle her voice.

"Tell me. What's going on?" I probe for a quick answer. *I'm late, I need to be out of here.*

"Mark's just been arrested." Her uncontrollable weeping voice is barely audible. We pause and I wait for an explanation before I push her further.

"For what, Paula? … Where are the kids? … I'd come instantly but I have to pick up my kids from soccer and music. I'll be there soon as I can. What are you going to do next?"

Her sobbing subsides. "I'm on my way home to be with the kids. Call me at home before you come; no … just come as soon as you can, okay?" I hear the disconnect click.

I hastily contemplate my options: I can pick up the kids and head for Tacoma. I have enough cash to buy hamburgers to feed them if I take them with me, or I can take them home, get them bathed, fed and settled before I take off.

Once long ago, I learned two heads are better than one when problems arise. Involve the family, consider their viewpoints, and let them share responsibility.

On the way home I explain the circumstances and offer the kids two choices, or I'm open for a better one. They take me up on staying home and putting themselves to bed. I will leave Aunt Paula's phone number on the fridge for any emergency.

I rush in the backdoor, shove the potatoes in the oven to give them a head start, get the boys started with showers, give directions to the girls concerning supper, then called Paula to let her know my progress.

The phone at her apartment rings several times before she picks it up. I can hear a combination of voices in the background.

"Paula? What's up?"

Paula's voice sounds strange. "Joella, some people here are from Child Protective Services. They want to take my babies away." She breaks down into deep wrenching sobs.

"Paula, what's going on? No, don't tell me, I'm on the way. Just don't say or do anything till I get there, okay? Have you called anyone else?"

"No," she weeps noisily. "Oh, Jo, it's all so terrible, I just don't know what to do."

I don't want my curious children upset so as relaxed as possible, I tell them, "I'll call you as soon as I find out what's happening, okay?" I blow kisses as I run out to the car, leaving a bewildered family behind to care for themselves.

The drive to Fife is impossible. Rush hour means we move at a snail's pace down a freeway with a seventy mile per hour speed limit. Inching along amidst several thousand cars headed south gives me time to think.

Paula didn't indicate her kids were in harms way; I didn't ask either. So why is Child Protective Services involved? Ever since Mark returned home, I've had a difficult time accepting him. Sometimes he's the same old Mark I'm used to but other times, he's moody and silent. Paula says it's because he doesn't feel well. I realize he's been in and out of the Seattle Veterans Hospital several times. They do tests and evaluate him but he always comes away with a clean bill of health. Until the next time and each time he's always sick enough to be admitted.

I arrived at Paula's one and a half hours later—a usual forty-five minute drive. There are two police cars parked outside the front of her apartment. I pushed my way through a crowd of spectators who have gathered and are conversing quietly in front of the apartment entrance.

"You a relative?" Someone asks.

"Yes, I'm her sister, please let me through." I push for an opening.

"CPS's here. They'se gonna take her kids away." Cigarette smoke trails from the nostrils of the lady informant. "I know of what I'm talkin', I'se been there."

Paula and Mark rented their apartment before he went overseas. When he returned home, with his medical condition he either uses Seattle Veterans Hospital or Madigan Hospital close by. My sister retained the residence, but to tell you the truth, I'm not comfortable in the neighborhood.

I worry about Paula and the kids—still babies—a two-year-old and a nine-month-old. Not the type of neighborhood I'd like them to grow up in.

The crowd allows me entrance. When I buzz the apartment, a man answers, "Yes?"

I'm tempted to say, "And who are you?" But instead, I announce myself, "Mrs. Simpson, Paula's sister. May I come in?" I hear the front door latch snap indicating that I'm allowed entrance.

I open a door to face a roomful of strangers. Paula has little Jeffrey in her arms and Tamara my niece, sees me and bursts across the room. "Annie Jo!" she screams. "Annie Jo! some policeman come and they took Daddy away and Mama had to come home from work. But this lady, she stayed with me till my mama come. Her name is … I surgot … I surgot what she told me." She clutches onto me as she timidly and shyly peers over at a young, long-haired, long-skirted, hippy-looking woman sitting on the couch.

I nod to her as I pick up Tammy on my way to stand beside Paula.

"The babies had anything to eat yet?" I loudly interrupt the conversation. No one bothers to acknowledge me or make introductions. "Paula? Isn't CPS here because of interest concerning the welfare of your children? *I don't know yet why they are here, it's time to find out.*"

"If you'll excuse me," I reach for baby Jeff and hold out my hand to Tammy, "I'm going to feed the children," I head for the kitchen.

The young CPS worker jumps up to follow me. A plain clothes, older gentleman, a deep frown etched on his leathery tanned face, intercepts us.

"Just a minute, Mrs. Markham." He directs his order to my sister. "Why don't you see to the children and we'll have a talk with your sister … what's your name?"

His face is so close to mine I fight the sensation to gag from the odor of his stale cigarette breath.

"We'll be right here with her if you need her, Mrs. Markham."

"Paula?" I insist. "Let me help you." I shove past the old man but not before he grabs my arm and draws me back into the room. I look around to see everyone is preoccupied and pretends not to notice the man's aggressive behavior.

I state firmly, "I know nothing of why you're here, your name, or what you want from me." I wrestle my arm from his grip. "Let me go."

Why am I being so belligerent? The man is only doing his duty. Maybe it's my reaction to jury duty under Judge Daly's superior attitude that has me upset.

The man opens with, "May I ask you some questions? I'm Detective O'Leary, Pat O'Leary. Mr. Mark Markham was arrested earlier this afternoon for rape charges."

It's a good thing he led me to a chair. *Mark? ... Lovable sick Mark? ... Who served as a Marine in Vietnam, served his country? ... Can't bring himself to talk about the atrocities of what he saw? ... Mark, who came home sick and no one knows why?*

I wanted to say ... "You have the wrong man."

"We're here waiting for the judge to send over papers to remove the children from these premises until Mr. Markham's case is settled."

"What?" I stammered. "He's in jail and you have to move the kids out? To where? Where did Mark ... by the way, Mark is an invalid ... are you aware of this? He should be in a military hospital. I shook my head vigorously—I can't make out any of this.

"Okay then, I'm next of kin," I said. "Doesn't that mean I have the right to take them? What about their other family, Mark's family? They're upright, upstanding citizens."

"I'm sorry, Tamara and Jeffrey will be under court protection until legal guardians are obtained for them. The State has wonderful foster care homes, the children will be given the best of care until the court decides for them.

"I know about foster homes, Mr. O'Leary, I'm a foster mother. So I'm eligible to take my niece and nephew, I'm licensed. Of course, you understand, I will have to turn the two boys in my care back to the State to make room for new children."

"Ma'am," he sputtered. *I can't help but notice every previously preoccupied face in the room is turned towards me.* "You're a foster mother? You have foster children in your home?"

Is he hard of hearing? "Yes, sir, I have two boys. We have four children of our own and by State Law we are allowed only six children under the roof at a time; however, there have been times our home was used for more than two foster boys, and I've never objected. It's you people who enforce the laws and Washington State Law forbids more than six children in a foster home.

"If I'm permitted to take family member children, you better believe I will. They come first. My home is already a foster home. I'm sure the court will find that I'm eligible to take my own kin, wouldn't you agree, sir?"

During an interval in our conversation, the young CPS caseworker entered the room.

"It's not our decision, Joella," *She addresses me as Joella, not Mrs. Simpson,* "as to where the children are placed, it's a matter for the court to decide. You may petition, but if your home is being used to capacity and you are next of kin, the court may feel it's not in the best interest of the children to place them with you. Consequences arise when family members ask to take children of criminals."

"Just a minute!" I shout. "Criminal! … You've already condemned Mark? From serving on jury duty, I was told the legal system, does not consider a person a criminal until they have been proven guilty. That's the reason for a jury … they must decide. You've already condemned Mark, my brother-in-law … he's not even had a trial. He's guilty you say? … I heard you both … you and Mr. O'Leary say so."

"No … oh, no," Mr. O'Leary flings up his arms in defense. "Molly Gollyway, uh … Miss Galloway, wasn't implying … someone accused Mr. Markham of rape, Mrs. Simpson. That's a serious charge, especially when the victim is a teenager. We have no choice but to put him under arrest. It's our duty to make sure his family—his children are safe. It's our duty to remove them from his home premises."

One of the police officers stepped forward. "Mrs. Simpson, do you folks have an attorney? You might want to contact one for legal information and of your *rights*."

My mind whirls. *Yes, we desperately need an attorney. We can't fight City Hall alone. This means Paula has no choice, she will have to let the children go with Miss Galloway, this young, inexperienced, know-it-all CPS worker.*

"At least these people have the decency to wait until we feed our children." Paula overheard the conversation between Mr. O'Leary, Miss Galloway, and myself.

"Jo," she whispers, "is it true we have no choice? Are they supposed to read us some *rights*? But what have we done that we need to know our legal rights?"

Officer O'Leary answers the buzz from outside to admit a police officer who comes in flashing some papers in his fist. Minutes later policemen on each side escort Miss Galloway with a shrieking Tammy in her arms and our tiny baby Jeffrey, too young to know what's happening, in the arms of Officer O'Leary. Everyone follows them out of the apartment while I hold my hysterical sister tight in my arms.

I wish with all my heart and soul I could erase my sister's burden, take away her pain. What had she done to deserve this? I'm still in a fog as to what's transpired.

A phrase comes to mind as I hold my uncontrollable weeping sister. 'Into each life some rain must fall.' *This isn't rain … it's hell and brimstone … it's live hot fire.*

My world is spinning out of control. I'm in the thick of deciding for the life of a woman who took away a man's life. Mark's charged with rape. What's going on?

"Paula," I reason with her, "you have to come home with me." I knew she would refuse.

I led her over to the couch, sat her down and explained a plan of action I felt best. She listened and showed interest when I said, "We don't have money for hiring attorneys to represent Mark or the children. We'll need to plead for a public defender."

Paula realized I'm right. People like us are not prepared to hire costly attorneys. People like us are supposed to believe we are innocent until proven guilty, but the courts aren't always merciful.

Paula and I both remember our heartbroken parents handing over precious land to the court. It had been bought legally and had authentic papers but they lacked enough funds to hire the best attorney.

The people gathered outside the front door are witnesses to the fact the wheels of justice don't always turn favorably for the less fortunate. Justice is not necessarily for those who tread in shoes of God's lesser people, they represent the more fortunate.

Paula slowly unraveled the story of Mark's arrest. This had happened during a bad day for him. "To pick up a little extra money, I did a double shift that day and asked the little fifteen-year-old girl down the street to watch the kids during the day. She knew them, I'd used her before.

"When I came home that night, Mark told me to never let that girl in our apartment again. He was the one who put the kids to bed, while the girl watched TV. He told her to go on home, the kids were in bed and he was going back to bed.

"After he went to bed, he told me, he started to sweat, sometimes he does this. So he took off all his clothes. He wasn't aware the girl hadn't left until she startled him by getting into bed with him. He said he was so weak and tired, he rolled away from her but she crawled over on top of him and started fondling and trying to kiss him. He told me this ... he said it was all he could do to throw her off of him and she fell on the floor.

"When I came home, he woke up and related all this. The girl must have gone home. She wasn't here when I arrived. I later gave the money to her mother because she wasn't at her home when I went to pay her. I've not seen her since.

"Jo, Mark is sick, he's miserable. I know there is something the matter but the doctors deny anything." Her voice little more than a whisper, "I think he's dying, Jo, and there's nothing I can do for him." Tears flooded her eyes and ran unchecked down her cheeks.

I'm amazed she has any tears left.

I decide for her. "You can't stay here alone. Go pack some clothes, I'll call your work and explain you need to get out of town for a few days. The CPS worker gave me phone numbers of contacts and there's nothing we can do tonight. I don't want you to be alone—you understand?"

In silence, I drove while Paula shed tears and wailed out her misery during the ride home.

"Tammy won't sleep a wink in a strange bed. Poor little Jeff, he won't recognize a familiar face ... they won't understand. Mark is just too sick to care about anything."

I let her cry, there was nothing I could do but be supportive.

I'm not sure what will greet me in my own home when we get there and tomorrow ... tomorrow there is no way out of my jury duty. If I were to miss, the case could be thrown out. I don't dare let my personal problems keep me away. It could mean a mistrial. Karin Colby has the right to my verdict. I took the responsibility on her behalf with no idea my private life would erupt while I served my jury duty.

The court is liable to throw me out for contempt; they could have me arrested for falsely representing myself. Unfortunately, I have few options before me.

CHAPTER 6

Tuesday, the fourth day of the trial. After a sleepless night, I face the day irritable. I was exhausted before last evening's catastrophe and it's anybody's guess how long my jury duty will last.

There is little I can do to help Paula, my traumatized sister. Her husband Mark—an invalid suffering from battle fatigue, a postwar syndrome from his 1968 tour of duty in Vietnam—has been arrested, charged with rape of a fifteen-year-old neighbor girl.

Their two small children were made wards of the court and are in foster care until the court and Social Welfare Department decide to reunite the family.

My husband and I whisper long into the night seeking a solution to the crisis. We will petition to take the children, if possible; however, we have little finances to assist Mark and Paula. They will have to request court appointed legal assistance.

~ ~ ~

Entering the courtroom, I sense but find it difficult to describe the atmosphere—tension, silent hostility and cold aloofness permeate the room. The defense attorney Mr. Dowd and the prosecuting attorney Mr. Clemens, appear removed from the surroundings, preoccupied with paperwork.

We perform the daily ritual of honoring Judge Daly, who ascends to his bench with an angry frown. *Oh-oh, today Nero's angry; Rome will burn. It doesn't appear our Judge Daly is in any mood for fiddle playin' 'round here.*

He glowers and growls for Mr. Dowd to make his opening statement in the second phase of the continuing trial against Karin Colby.

Karin's shaved head appears out of place. She is above average in height and her muscular build gives her a masculine rather than feminine outward appearance.

Mary Alice and I exchange glances and shrug our shoulders at the judge's demeanor. My two aspirins taken earlier are no longer working.

Mr. Dowd arises from his chair and begins. "You," he addresses the jury, "may have wondered why I haven't shown more concern for my client, Miss Colby, during the first phase of the trial that decided her guilt."

Mr. Dowd describes how the system with its dual trial has put his client and himself at a disadvantage. "An impossible position ... it's unfeasible for my client to be judged fairly.

"For two reasons." He emphasizes by striking one fist into the palm of his other hand. "For two reasons," he repeats, "her innocence ... her insanity ... neither were allowed to be mentioned as evidence. The court refused to allow us to be heard."

He looked at each of us. "Okay, let's put the first part of the trial behind us. I'm counting on you to hear the new evidence in this case with an open mind."

First, Mr. Dowd gestures toward his client, then walks over to the defense table and places his hand on Karin Colby's shoulder.

Karin is calm and at ease, even smiles up at Mr. Dowd. She appears happy even though we declared her guilty of murder.

I feel anxious. Glancing around at my fellow jurors, they too seem nervous, a bit unsettled.

If she is insane, I'm sorry for her. However, I find her emotionally content attitude sordid.

A stir in the gallery at the back of the room draws our attention to the Oriental family making themselves known with angry mumbling.

Mr. Dowd senses the friendly camaraderie contact between him and Karin Colby isn't appealing to some people. He avoids acknowledging the intrusion from the back of the room by abruptly turning back to the jurors.

"The molding of Karin Colby's life, before her decision to study Zen Buddhism," Mr. Dowd looks from one to the other of us, "began when Karin turned five-years-old. Her father was diagnosed with a chronic mental illness and distanced himself from the girl. She grew up knowing little concerning her father.

"Karin's early training was at the discretion of several babysitters. When she began having problems at school, her parents simply removed her and sent her to another school.

"Karin's scholastic grades and IQ tests were exceptionally high. Each school she attended indicated she was above average, a well-adjusted bright child. However, between the eighth and eleventh grades, her scores went from high to near failing. Her teachers commented, 'She was withdrawn and apathetic.'

"This young woman's situation," Mr. Dowd suggested, "was never dealt with properly. Number one: instead of changing schools, it would have been much better for her to have stayed in one place. Number two: the relationship between her and her mother was too intense. And number three: neither parent nor any personnel of the schools she attended considered that Karin needed counseling.

"In fact, Mrs. Colby, by her own admission, told the schools that Karin was just going through what girls outgrow … a rebellious phase. She referred to Karin's problems as simply what she thought all kids went through.

"Though her grades were poor and her home life miserable, Karin tested high on the Washington State pre-college exams and was accepted into the University of Washington School of Medicine. It was while attending the *U-dub*, she found religion.

"At first she was enthusiastic about the Unitarian Church but soon lost interest in the casualness and inattentiveness of the organization.

She didn't get along with members of the Christian Science Church, or the Church of Scientology.

"It was when she met a member of the Kirkland Zen Foundation and began visiting there that Zen Buddhism appealed to her. It promised absolute spiritual enlightenment. Karin felt she could now end her search for a church and religion. There, as a woman, she was accepted as equal and treated with respect for her gender.

"She began attending the meditation sessions, then signed up for the course. After that she moved into the establishment and became a resident in order to practice Zen full time. She worked in the kitchen to meet her board and room expenses.

"I had the opportunity," Mr. Dowd said, "to speak with a witness from the Zen Foundation, who described Karin as 'being overly obsessive and self-absorbed; it was as if she was in her own world or universe.'

"When Karin and the other students heard that the impressive Zen Master, Nishimura, was coming to lead a group through the intensive winter session, Karin felt she was ready to attend the harsh schedule of the retreat.

"Karin's drive ... her goal ... was to solve the riddle. A riddle and means to solve it, that as I understand it, is irrational by design—long demanding hours of sitting cross-legged without moving a muscle, strenuous body discipline, as well as enduring the alleged prodding and being struck with a heavy oak stick.

"I wish for the evidence," Mr. Dowd explained, "to show that the witness you heard the other day failed to mention, or didn't think it important to mention, a detail he left out ... so you heard only part of the puzzle.

"I'd like to read an excerpt." Mr. Dowd retrieved a book from his desk, opened it to a bookmarked page and read in a loud, clear voice:

"The Zen Master Lin-chi was once asked by a monk, 'What would you do if you were going somewhere and you suddenly met the Buddha in the road? Lin-chi answered, 'If you meet the Buddha in the road and he stands in your way, kill him! If you meet the great Zen teachers of the past, kill them! If you meet your parents, kill them! That is the only way to be free.'"

I thought our audible gasps at hearing the full horrifying Zen Master command would disturb Judge Daly, who continued writing and paid little attention to the reading.

Mr. Dowd's frown, I'm sure, is the result of Judge Daly's inattentiveness but he continues. "Karin was repeatedly advised by the students and the Zen Master Nishimura that her one goal, her whole reason for enduring the painful retreat schedule, was to solve her riddle. Only by solving the puzzle could she be enlightened. Some advice, wouldn't you say? I leave it to you to decide. Where did it lead her?"

Hands joined behind his back, Mr. Dowd patiently balanced heel to toe back and forth as if allowing us time to digest what he just fed us.

Mr. Dowd abruptly halted, turned toward us and stated, "Evidence will show that Miss Colby suffers from chronic schizophrenia, a severe mental illness."

He looked at each juror to assure he made personal individual contact. It isn't difficult to respect his effort.

I feel as though I'm a child and Mr. Dowd assumes I'm not ... or, we the jury, aren't paying attention unless he keeps an eye on us. He's trying his best to defend his client, but his method isn't very effective. Maybe Karin should tell her own story, Mr. Dowd, your technique doesn't sit well with me.

"To sum it up," he addresses us under his continuous stare, "the extreme brutal discipline and humiliating rituals endured during this meditation retreat, along with the confusing moral environment practiced by the Zen religion, didn't challenge Miss Colby's pre-existing mental illness ... only aggravated it and drove her out of her mind. She became insane ... disoriented ... she experienced her first acute psychotic incident.

"Karin Colby lost her ability to distinguish the difference between symbolic and real gestures. She killed a man thinking she'd rightfully answered the puzzle.

"An expert witness in psychiatry will testify that my client didn't understand what she was doing, that it wasn't acceptable, and she still does not understand. There isn't a better explanation for the legal definition of insanity." Mr. Dowd turned, walked back to his table and plunked the book down with a pronounced thud before saying, "No further questions, Your Honor."

My problem is, I don't like aggressive people. I'm resisting Mr. Dowd's argument for the same reason. He is right, but I don't like pushy people, especially pushy women.

Judge Daly looks up from his business at hand and invites the prosecutor Mr. Clemens to speak next.

Mr. Clemens has not improved his appearance; the man's desk is a testimony; it resembles a cluttered room—papers scattered about with books lying open. Using his hands on the table for leverage, he raises himself to a standing position.

He smiles at us. *I'm glad he doesn't feel it's necessary to stand right in front of the jury box to stare us down as is Mr. Dowd's technique.*

In his easy drawl with a gentle smile, he states, "Ah guess ... the only thing Ah kin add at this point is ... the better you kin understand the legal concept of insanity, the guiltier Karin Colby appears. If she's gonna be acquitted, then Miss Colby hasta prove that because of her mental disease ... or defect, she had no notion what she was doin' when she killed her teacher."

Mr. Clemens chuckles. "The evidence shows me that Miss Colby absolutely knew what she was doin'. Why ... she beat the life right outta that man ... far's ah'm concerned."

The room retained a difficult silent amusement.

Mr. Clemens paused then said, "Ah don't know 'bout ya'll but my stomach's growlin' so loud hits disturbin' ma hearin' anymore testimony. Ah move we adjourn till Ah feed maself a bite a lunch."

I couldn't help but note Judge Daly's pleased approval. His mouth almost broke into a grin, enough so the frown he'd brought into the room disappeared. He seconded the prosecutor's suggestion and adjourned the court until two o'clock.

I just happened to look over and witness a scowl on Mr. Dowd's face. I'm sure he didn't enjoy seeing the *good ole boy* rapport between Mr. Clemens and Judge Daly.

Mr. Dowd's job isn't easy; I feel for him having to defend a destructive young woman. Too bad he doesn't possess Mr. Clemens' southern charm. To tell the truth, poor Mr. Dowd is an obnoxious man but that has nothing to do with Karin.

I politely decline Mary Alice's suggestion we eat lunch outside.

Should I call home or wait? I've been fortunate to tune out my domestic problems all morning. I'm going to wait. There's nothing I can do from here but get upset.

I'm still undecided whether to approach the bench or just wait till I'm summoned into the judge's chamber when they find out my deceptive circumstances. Maybe policemen will come to the house, put me in handcuffs in front of the kids and lead me away, like they did Mark.

My mother's answer to such a question would be 'Fools rush in where angels fear to tread.' Think I'll adopt her philosophy for now; I'll wait for them to come to me.

My husband usually leaves for work by two p.m. so he is there all morning to drive Paula around if she needs transportation or to help her get organized. We drove home in my car last night so she's without wheels.

I left her a list of phone numbers to make necessary appointments; tomorrow, she has the use of my car.

I wasn't in the mood to join the others, make small talk and chew on a bland, dry sandwich. The pressure and stress of life is getting to me.

I passed through the courthouse doorway facing Fourth Avenue. I need a breath of fresh air. *What I really need are some instructions for Karin's meditation exercises.*

I meander down to the street crossing in the direction of the Smith Tower building. At one time the Tower was the tallest building west of the Mississippi.

Waiting for the light to change, I glance up to the top of the structure where I once walked around the circle to observe the city from every angle. *It's been years since I'd made the climb.*

I pay the fare for the elevator ride and appease myself with the notion, *Who knows how long my jury duty will last, especially with my family crisis rearing its ugly head? I'll treat myself while I'm downtown … memories of my last excursion to the top of the Smith Tower to pacify my mind when they haul me off to jail.*

I depart the elevator with groups and couples interested in the spectacular site. We gaze out at a city far changed from when I first viewed it in 1955. The Space Needle built in 1962 for the World's Fair may be taller but it would be impossible to access in a lunchtime hour.

Four prominent Seattle hills rise from Elliot Bay and surrounding areas: Queen Anne Hill to the north, the Denny Regrade to the northeast, Capitol Hill extends from the waterfront east and Beacon Hill to the south.

From the waterfront west, connected by a bridge, is the Magnolia District with Ballard, Seattle's little Scandinavia, situated in the vicinity of Queen Anne Hill. North and northeast, the University district sprawls to the shores of Lake Washington on the east and south to the Denny Regrade—the hill Seattle downsized by washing it into Elliot Bay. Ferries and pleasure craft fill the bay waters. Freight trains move in and out of the busy port city. Three freeways move traffic in, out, and around the big city to suburban areas.

At the foot of Beacon Hill to the south is the Oriental or International District, known for the longest flume in the Pacific Northwest—built to skid logs into the bay. Logging, now a thing of the past, districts surrounding that area are still referred to as *Skid Row*, as famous as the Bowery of New York and San Francisco's Barbary Coast.

Bridges join Seattle's hills and districts. At the foot of Queen Anne, the Hiram Chittenden Locks transfer salt and fresh water vessels of all sizes and description back and forth into and out of Lake Union and Lake Washington.

I watch two gleaming, white ferry boats slowly pass each other in blue Puget Sound waters, sailing to and from Bremerton, home of the big naval shipyard, and Vashon Island, a thriving farm community.

Many people who live on the Islands commute to Seattle for work. They drive the Tacoma Narrows Bridge or take the ferries. The ferries not only haul vehicles and passengers but freight trucks headed for other cities across the sound and west over the Hood Canal Bridge and up the long stretch of highway to Port Townsend and on to the coast and beaches of the Pacific Northwest.

Seattle is a diversified city. Built on hills, as is Rome and patterned after San Francisco. It features fairytale gingerbread trimmed architectural mansions as well as government housing projects, remnants of World War Two when the city boomed with government workers. After the war, the project houses were purchased by the city to house low-income families. Housing developments grace the hillsides and suburbs with manicured, beauty-barked yards filled with native trees, shrubs and flowers.

Seattle sits like a jewel surrounded by blue water. She's neither glitzy nor brown and brittle, but a soft inviting, luscious, evergreen town warmed under a comfortable sun, when it shines.

I summarize Seattle as a friendly city with dignity and aged beauty—a cultural city interested in its educational development and fine arts.

This is my city. It has its share of cops and robbers, but each district boasts of playfields and well-tended parks. To the east of Capitol Hill lies a large arboretum put together by women in the early nineteen-hundreds, who donated a great variety of flora from their world travels abroad. Volunteer Park sits atop the hill with a museum and an exotic plant conservatory, and beside the park resides the oldest cemetery in Seattle.

A glance at my watch tells me I have to hurry to make it back to court on time. I feel better after this break from the confinement and doldrums of the trial and my stressful night, but I do wonder—*How much longer will I be a juror when my home situation comes to light?*

CHAPTER 7

Wednesday, the fifth day of trial. The jury patiently waits while Judge Daly on his royal throne fusses with his robe, restacks piles of papers on his desk then requests something from the clerk before he's satisfied and looks up to greet us.

"Please," he instructs Mr. Dowd, "call your first witness for the defense."

The witness reminds me of my grandmother's garden variety references used to describe people. In her tongue, this man is a lean, lanky, pole-bean of a fellow with a pointed goatee attached to his chin.

At first, I mistook the witness seated at Mr. Dowd's table for a student, mislead by his college league sports jacket and horn-rimmed glasses. But on his way to take the witness stand, his receding hairline gave me to know otherwise. I'm sure he's approximately my age, not younger.

He introduces himself as Dr. Leopold Jarbouski, a Psychiatrist at the University of Washington Neurological Research Department. After a lengthy and dull verbal résumé of his background and qualifications, he tells us he specializes in the treatment and study of schizophrenia, a mental disorder.

Dr. Jarbouski testifies, "I met with Karin Colby several times since her arrest for murder and have administered a number of psychological tests."

When Mary Alice glances my way, I roll my eyes as Dr. Jarbouski goes into great detail to explain results from the many tests. His medical jargon is foreign to us lay people, who are supposedly Karin's equal or peers.

I find it difficult to follow Dr. Jarbouski's review of test after test. My mind wanders to my sister Paula's circumstance. I wonder, *Is Paula's Mark provided with psychiatric treatment through the military? I've heard that when new medical methods and treatments are developed, the military medical division employs them to aid the severely wounded. I hope and pray this is true for Mark's sake.*

When Dr. Jarbouski finished describing his tests, Mr. Dowd began his questions. We, the jurors, come up out of our stupor or trance to focus on Mr. Dowd's interrogation.

"And were you able, Dr. Jarbouski," Mr. Dowd asked, "to make a conclusive diagnosis?"

Dr. Jarbouski attempts a condescending smile. "I suppose you could say … you must understand that until we can positively identify chemicals and neurobiological components of all thoughts and feelings, no psychiatric diagnosis will ever be *absolutely* conclusive."

Dr. Jarbouski stares straight ahead, his long fingers tented in front of his chest. "I find it is not difficult to evaluate Miss Colby's history, symptoms, or behavior patterns; they are all consistent with the diagnosis of her mental disorder."

Mr. Dowd, looks at the jury as he asks, "And what is that?"

"It's a progressive illness known as chronic undifferentiated schizophrenia."

"Dr. Jarbouski, might you explain … in layman's terms … what that means?"

Dr. Jarbouski showed a bit of pleasure in being asked to explain. He scooted to the edge of his chair and grabbed onto the railing in front of him as he explained.

"Most of us are comfortable with people we can depend on, people who are predictable. Schizophrenia is a disease that makes its victims unpredictable.

"If you observe the disorder carefully, you realize the symptoms aren't unpredictable. But the average person doesn't know enough about schizophrenia to understand the symptoms.

"First," Dr. Jarbouski paused, "yes … as I was saying, first of all … it's important to know that Miss Colby's father was diagnosed as a schizophrenic. We are certain this disease has a genetic factor … or component." Reaching down into his briefcase beside his chair, he withdrew several documents and commenced to read aloud facts relating to Karin's father's medical history. He painstakingly put away the documents, turned to face the jurors and said, "Schizophrenic symptoms begin to show themselves in early adolescence.

"For most of us, adolescence is a horrible, frustrating time." He grimaces. "I know, I speak from experience." His laugh fails to draw our response.

"We are forced into … maybe better words are *try out* … forced to try out new phases in our lives. We break away from our families in our attempt to discover who we are.

"It's a struggle to determine who we really are. For instance, why do we act one way to our friends and treat our parents another way? Who is the real me? It's a traumatic stressful stage of life for us. Fortunately, most of us survive, settle down and by our twenties, we're comfortable with our roles in life."

I'm amused how he nodded in agreement with himself. As if he's pleased he's done an excellent job presenting his testimony.

He finished by telling us, "Schizophrenics are never comfortable with themselves even when they get older. Their confusion only becomes more intense. Schizophrenics sense themselves with such terrifying intensity that, in light of their self-awareness, they lose their spontaneity. It's like … you and I suffering a bad case of stage fright, but imagine, if you will, having it all the time."

I'm sure the other jurors, as myself, find the concept unpleasant. I'm sure we all have had self-conscious monster moments like he just described. But imagine, day after day facing panic, anger and despair.

Dr. Jarbouski didn't help our imagination as he continued. "The disease worsens, the patient's thoughts get mixed up. Imagine, if you will, thinking of something positive while all the time your feelings are depressed with sadness. It can become such a strong sense with schizophrenics, they actually think they hear voices commanding them from outside their bodies. They think they are being commanded by God, the devil, or someone of authority. These unfortunate folks become withdrawn, shy … they have lost their self-control.

"They become nervous, scared recluses; they are far from dangerous. Like turtles, if you will, they pull back in their shells. Occasionally … occasionally ... a schizophrenic will become so overwhelmed they have a psychotic episode and lose their self-control entirely."

"So tell the jury," Mr. Dowd spoke up, "do you suggest that Karin Colby had just such an episode when she killed Mr. Nishimura, her Zen Master?"

To emphasize his affirmation, Dr. Jarbouski rapped his first finger against the railing and nodded his head vigorously. "Absolutely! Once she slipped into the state of mind … psychotic episode … there was nothing she could do to break the cycle. She was helplessly out of control."

Dr Jarbouski gazed above him, his head poised at an angle like he was searching the air for the right word. "Once she became psychotic … she lost all sense of reality, all self-control."

Dr. Jarbouski paused again, then suddenly his face lit up, he leaned back in his chair, crossed one leg over the other, his left hand resting on his right ankle. "It's like," his face shined with delight, "it's like getting caught up in a whirlpool. Once you get caught in the current, there is no escape. It pulls you down. You have nowhere to go but down, there is no getting out of its force. There is nothing strong enough or fast enough to pull you out of its centrifugal spin.

"This is what happens to a schizophrenic, once the psychotic part of them takes over … that person you think should *know better* … that nice person … the person their friends and family know … that person can no longer resist the forces. Their mind is thrown into confusion. They are being manipulated; there is nothing to hold onto, everything around them is chaos."

We follow Dr. Jarbouski's gaze over to Karin Colby, who is rapidly writing on one of Mr. Dowd's yellow legal pads. The doctor then turned to face the jury. "We who are not afflicted by the disease should be grateful we don't know what it feels like."

My brother-in-law Mark has been diagnosed with a mental disorder. I wonder ... is it possible he's suffering from a condition much like the doctor just described?

What if Mark's brain is damaged from the Agent Orange contamination? Is it possible he is passing into a whirlpool or has he come out of one? Would he be the same as before or is everything around him changed? How has his mind been altered? We, his family, know he's not the same as before he went overseas.

Is it possible Mark did rape the neighbor girl; that he was suffering a psychotic phase? If he's successfully treated, does this mean his life can be changed back to how we knew him before?

What about Karin? Can she be changed? She's a killer, someone who took a man's life. But with treatment, can she become a healthy, reasonable woman?

My heart aches for these young people, Mark and Karin ... Karin, especially. She looks pathetic more than guilty of murder to me. And Mark, does Mark know what he did? Does he understand?

Dr. Jarbouski draws my attention. "During Karin's psychotic episode at the church, she suddenly found herself swept up in a delirium to the correct answer the Zen Master requested. The answer to the puzzle— kill the Buddha in the road. And so she attacked the Zen Master with the man's own staff."

The doctor continued, "A variety of situations can bring on these psychotic episodes. Sometimes they occur without an apparent reason, but most often are ignited by emotional and stressful situations. For instance, a visit to one's parents' home or having to ride a public bus and being stared at, or having to take part in any social circumstance that makes one feel more self-conscious than usual."

Mr. Dowd asked, "Then would you suggest that the Zen retreat might ... could have ... triggered Karin Colby's psychotic episode?"

Dr. Jarbouski laughed out loud, shook his head and with the utmost bitter expression on his face said, "Mr. Dowd, I find it difficult to believe that you or I could participate in activities like Miss Colby endured without a breakdown. If you ask me, this is precisely what most so-called religious experiences are, episodes of nervous tension provoked by sensory deprivation, extreme—"

"Objection!" Mr. Clemens roared. "The doctor's opinion concernin' what he claims is normal religious experiences isn't relevant, Yer Honor. It's biasin' the jury against the religion Miss Colby chooses ta practice."

Judge Daly's bushy eyebrow lifts. "Sustained," he declared and followed his statement with a sigh of boredom.

Dr. Jarbouski's reaction is no more than a shrug. He doesn't appear upset and continues. "It's quite common for these exhausted people to experience hallucinations and interpret those hallucinations as deep insight, visions of God's divine commands.

"There is no doubt in my mind," Dr. Jarbouski strongly emphasized, "that the retreat *did* trigger Miss. Colby's psychosis.

"And frankly," he added, "from my professional point of view on the activities of this retreat … put it this way if you will … it wouldn't take an evil genius to create an atmosphere more deadly and likely to bring on a psychotic episode in a schizophrenic."

"Could you be more explicit, Doctor?" Mr. Dowd requested. "What specifically about this retreat … and I use your quote, Doctor … '*did* trigger Miss. Colby's' psychotic behavior?"

"Well," Dr. Jarbouski stated, "just about everything. Oh, I see … yes, let me be more specific.

"Let's begin with sensory deprivation. Imagine sitting hours and hours a day cross-legged while meditating without moving. This means barring any outside sounds, sights or smells that could interfere with your thoughts or enter your mind.

"There is total silence, no talking or moving about for long periods of time. And then the students are allowed only four or five hours of sleep. They are awakened at four a.m. every morning and move around in their silent world. It would make anyone suffer from delusions, but it upsets the schizophrenic in a much shorter time.

"Imagine, if you will, after getting to the meditation hall, you are required to do a series of one hundred prostrations in front of an image of Buddha, even before you are required to go into the cross-legged meditation.

"So … these participants suffer from sleep deprivation and repetitive motor activities which leads to disorganized thinking and increased hypnotic suggestions. Oh, and don't forget the concentration needed for the puzzle they are supposed to be solving."

Dr. Jarbouski shook his head violently a couple of times before he continued. "I've actually been told that Zen students are led to believe that if they solve these puzzles they will have profound insights into the *true nature* of the universe, which presumably answers all their questions about the meaning of life and whatever.

"These puzzles make no sense whatsoever. And apparently that is their point. I believe I mentioned *disorganized thinking*. It's the key to defining schizophrenia. What could be more stressful than for a student who has the disease, to engage in rigorous exercises that are created for the purpose of bypassing conventional notions of reality?

"These Zen exercises," Dr. Jarbouski emphasized, "are carried out in an atmosphere of severe discipline, allowing no relaxation of one's will or self-control and the poor student has very little of this in the first place."

The expression that crossed the doctor's face is almost despairing as he shook his head. "Then there's the fact that the Zen Master is a spiritual authority and that his spiritual vision allows him to interpret all the illusions we ordinary people live under.

"He's presumably an authority on false pretences and claims to understand the very nature of the universe. He claims he knows you better than you know yourself.

"Tell me, wouldn't someone with a deep fear of seeming thin-skinned or false feel provoked by such an authority? Wouldn't you be terrified? I know I would be terrified of being discovered to be, and positively identified as, a spiritual social failure. Add to this the right—tradition they call it—for a Zen Master to strike students with a huge, heavy wooden stick as punishment for making noise or unnecessary movement. The situation becomes even more frightening.

"The moment Karin started to lose control by crying and laughing and the Zen Master struck her with the stick, she simply became hysterical; at that moment, that point, the blow from the stick left her without sense of what she was doing."

Dr. Jarbouski gave us cause to believe that since Mr. Nishimura was an Oriental Zen Master, a Buddha, Karin reasoned that the master was some sort of apparition, a spirit of Buddha and his behavior described the puzzle. Karin played the role. She must have repeated the puzzle to herself many times over the four days of retreat.

"In this circumstance, who knows what path extreme psychological distress will take? In Karin's mind, she felt it was coming from the universe itself—from God.

"In any case," the doctor summed up his argument, "Karin believed at that time and moment, and still believes, that she did the right thing—the only thing she could do. And she had the moral force, according to the Zen Master teachings, of the universe to back her up. That is why she has no sense of remorse. Her sense of reality is utterly inconsistent with what she understands is reality."

The jury watched Mr. Dowd nod smartly before turning towards the counsel table, then stop and half turn to face the doctor. "Dr. Jarbouski, was Karin aware she was killing the man when she swung the heavy stick?"

Dr. Jarbouski blinked before he said, "No, not in any practical sense. What happened at that moment, on that day, has no substance or reality. It was kinda like a dream … better yet … a nightmare. She was no more in control of herself than we are of our dreams."

Mr. Dowd indicated he was through questioning the witness. Judge Daly excused Dr. Jarbouski and followed by consulting his watch and the wall clock. He then announced, "We weren't able to recess for morning break, so let's adjourn for lunch until one p.m."

I stand at attention while *Caesar* Judge Daly gathers his robe and papers before majestically retiring from his throne to his private chamber.

I stifle my amusement envisioning Judge Daly's imaginary olive wreath halo a bit askew over one bushy eyebrow as he exits the room. *Did I imagine it, or was he unusually quiet this morning?*

CHAPTER 8

While in the restroom, Mary Alice and I plan to avoid Mike. She opens the door and scans the hallway in both directions before we make a dash for the stairs. We're confident Mike isn't one to take the stairs.

Outside the building, a blue, cloudless sky stretches to eternity. The brightness and heat of midday would have been overpowering, if not for a cool breeze sweeping up the hill off the Sound.

We follow with others to a patch of lawn at one side of the King County courthouse where benches have been placed here and there for public use. Homeless citizens lounging or napping on the grass away from us use their backpacks and bedrolls for headrests.

My dry sandwich lacks taste. The orange I'd quartered is withered and juiceless. Fresh air and sun make up for my pitiful lunch.

Mary Alice lifts one end of her sandwich inspecting the interior. "I don't know how people stand sandwiches day after day. I hate mayonnaise but what else is there to hold the insides in the bread?"

I suggest, "You could always bring a roasted turkey leg to gnaw on."

"Hey," she said, "did you notice our *Roman Highness* Daly? He acted strange this morning. I got the feeling *Big Bird* wasn't his usual arrogant self."

"Maybe it had to do with Dr. J. That man drives me nuts with all his minute details. I wanna yell at him, 'Get to the point. What is your point?' But, he does seem to know about an abnormal mind."

"Judge Daly," Mary Alice continues, "is out of his element. He's in the wrong time slot."

"Which means?"

"Doubt he's ever heard of the Emancipation Proclamation; it's too new for him. Bet his family owned thousands of slaves and he's used to people trembling in their boots when they're around him. Puts up a good front, like he thrives on the smell of fear, glandular and otherwise, especially from the lower class."

"You mean you figure he's really a pussycat," I interject, "and Dr. *Jabber*, or whatever, scares our noble judge?"

"Yep." Mary Alice nods. "I think he's afraid to let his guard down for fear of a moment that will expose his unholy, uncharacteristic weakness. He doesn't want to be caught off guard, undefended. He's afraid the good doctor will discover this and take advantage of his enfeeblement."

Mary Alice surprises me with her clever diagnostic stereotyping of *Caesar* Daly, who then must endure a dual personality."

I wish I could bare my soul to Mary Alice. I wish I knew what to expect if and when my criminal act is discovered concerning my brother-in-law's Vietnam condition.

We return to the courtroom refreshed. I stifle a nagging sensation I should call home. There is little I can do about the home situation from here. *One thing at a time,* I conclude, *one step at a time.*

Waiting for Judge Daly, I give thought to whether Karin Colby was insane when she committed the murder. It seemed to me that if she were in the state of mind Dr. Jarbouski described, then it is believable and conceivable she could kill someone without understanding what she was doing. *I've never done anything in a dream but isn't this what Dr. Jarbouski described as Karin's condition? 'She was wide awake but she moved and her action was as if in a dream.' How long would such an episode last … a few seconds … longer? After she hit the Zen Master, wouldn't she have snapped out of her dream?*

I no more understand Dr. Jarbouski's strategy than I can will my heart to stop or quit breathing. I'm truly lost.

The afternoon begins with Judge Daly's attitude friendlier. He explains, "It's time to hear the cross-examination."

Mr. Clemens, from his table asks, "Dr. Jarbouski ... now hep me if ya will, sir, ta understand. Which of the psychological tests did ya say was given ta the defendant that confirmed her diagnosis of schizophrenia?"

We look over to Dr. Jarbouski, who smiles as if he anticipated the question. "Mr. Clemens, there are no tests that can absolutely confirm a diagnosis of schizophrenia. The disorder is determined from behavior and response to treatment."

"Ah see," Mr. Clemens mumbles aloud for the jury's benefit. He rose slowly with the aid of his table and walked to the front of the witness stand. "And, Dr. Jarbouski, Ah need more hep. Ah don't quite understand about insanity ... is there a test ... any test atall ... ta confirm a positive diagnosis of insanity? Would ya enlighten me here, Doctor?"

"No, sir. Insanity is a legal term, not a medical term. It's up to the court to decide if she's legally insane or not."

The prosecutor nodded politely and said in his soothing southern dialect, "Yes, well thank ya, sir ... Ah was just about ta git ta that part."

Mr. Clemens waddled back to the table, searched through a jumble of papers, picked up his briefcase and removed a sheet of paper. "Here 'tis ... this here's a report published by the American Psychiatric Association. Ya'll familiar with this organization, Dr. Jarbouski?" Mr. Clemens looks over his shoulder towards the doctor.

"Yes, sir, their reports are very thorough and quoted from often."

"Good ... then let me read ta ya." Mr. Clemens clears his throat noisily. "It says here, 'The line between an irresistible impulse and an impulse not resisted is probably no sharper than the line between twilight and dusk.' Are we on the same page, Doctor?"

"In theory, yes," the doctor admits.

"Thank ya, Dr. Jarbouski. Now ... if Ah may—" Mr. Clemens selects a sheet of paper from the table. "This here publication ... report, if ya will ... is by the American Bar Association. Ya'll familiar with the American Bar Association, Dr. Jarbouski? Good ... it says here," Mr. Clemens holds his head higher and adjusts his glasses to read: 'Experience confirms that there is still no accurate scientific basis for measurin' one's capacity for self-control or for calibratin' the impairment of such capacity. There is, in short, no objective basis for distinguishin' between offenders who are deterrable and those who are undeterred, between the impulse that was irresistible and the impulse not to resist, or between substantial impairment of capacity and some lesser impairment. The question then remains unanswerable or, at best, can be answered only by moral guesses.'"

Mr. Clemens looks up from the paper and over toward the doctor. Without confrontation, he asks, "What about this, Doctor? Does it make sense … does it sound right ta ya, sir?"

Dr. Jarbouski isn't relaxed but keeps his composure. "I have no choice but to agree that there is no absolute objective basis for telling the difference … yes."

It's obvious to the jury, Dr. Jarbouski isn't pleased with how the testimony is proceeding.

Mr. Clemens nodded then said, "So … Dr. Jarbouski, ya'll bein' a professional man an all … all this means," he holds up and rattles the paper, "is that in the absence of a conclusive medical diagnosis of insanity … it's the moral sense of the jurors that decides. Do Ah read this correctly, Doctor? Ya'll agree, sir?"

"Objection!" Mr. Dowd cries out. "This line of reasoning is gratuitous. He's trying to invalidate the doctor's testimony by asking him legal-philosophy questions, not medical questions."

Judge Daly's eyebrow lifts when he orders, "Sustained, Mr. Dowd, please sit down." We watch his eyebrow lower.

Mr. Clemens bows his head towards his opponent in a gesture of penitence before he resumes his questioning. "Now … tell us, if ya will, Dr. Jarbouski," he faced the doctor, "is it true … in yer esteemed estimation … that criminals who are not insane … but have personality disorders that made 'em violently antisocial without any sense of remorse … are they responsible for what they've done?"

Dr. Jarbouski blurts out before Mr. Clemens finished, "Oh, certainly I agree … that's a different type of illness though … but yes."

"Then, Doctor, the reason Ah'm mentionin' this is … Ah want ta git it clear for the court, ya understand … mental illness by itself does not automatically make a man legally insane … now does it?"

"Objection!" Mr. Dowd protested rising from his chair. "Your Honor, the prosecutor is testifying, not questioning."

"Sustained," Judge Daly confirmed.

I wish the defense attorney would let Karin get up on the witness stand. I wonder if the other jurors, like myself, would feel better able to judge from listening to her and watching her react?

The testimony so far intrigues me … the suggestion that trying to make a boundary between an irresistible impulse and an impulse not resisted and the reference to them being like twilight and dusk is a crucial point.

It's a fact that we all think we can tell when someone is mentally ill or psychologically out of control. An inappropriate comment, an awkward movement or an inappropriate facial expression, these are clues, but are we experienced at identifying mental illness?

Judge Daly told us at the beginning of the trial that the defendant does not have to testify and Mr. Dowd informed us that sometimes it serves justice better to let the evidence speak on behalf of the accused, rather than speaking for themself.

On the way back to his table, Mr. Clemens nodded toward Judge Daly. "The prosecution rests, Yer Honor."

Judge Daly announced, "We will hear further cross-examination tomorrow and so ends our day."

My day in court, that is. On the ride home I fight to stay awake. I'm exhausted. I've yet to fix dinner, kids to pick up, homework to oversee, and my sister and her problems to deal with before I can call it a day.

I slowly climb the steps, open the front door and I'm enveloped by the wonderful aroma of roast beef and overwhelmed with the fragrance from fresh baked bread.

"Hello," I call from the foyer. "Fee, fie, foe, fum, I smell the—"

"In here," my sister answers from the back of the house.

Wending my way through the living room and dining area, I enter the kitchen. "So, what took place for you today?" I ask of the form bending over the open oven door that exposes a succulent roast surrounded with carrots, potatoes and onions.

Paula ladles broth drippings from the roast over the veggies and shoves all back into the oven depths before she stands up. "My brother-in-law Glen is a genius, sis. He knows everyone and everybody. Tomorrow, I have appointments galore."

"What do you know about the kids, Paula?" My sister's relaxed poise comes as a surprise.

"You guys know the family they're with and though I'm not to have contact with them, your friends have invited me to drop by with cookies—a friendly call, you understand, and I'm to see my kids. Tammy and Jeff are together, thank goodness, and they sounded happy in the background when Glen let me talk to Mrs. Steve. Well, actually, when he called Mrs. Steve, she talked with me. It's not easy for me, Jo, but it's nice to know my kids are okay and in good hands."

"Oh, how fortunate you have Mrs. Steve. I'm glad. If anything were to happen to Glen or me, I'd want our kids to stay in such a home. They are the dearest people. Raised five of their own, you know, and probably over a hundred other kids by now.

"And Mark? How's Mark doing or have you heard?"

"I'm worried about him … he says he's running a temperature; he's upset." She gestures with palms outspread, her shoulders hunched. "But, what can I do … what can we expect?"

I know my sister, she's doing a good job covering her fears and maintaining her composure.

"You look beat." She studies me.

"I am, but I'll feel much better with some of this wonderful smelling food inside me. I'm starved. I'm not a good sandwich maker, never have been, so my lunches taste like crap. But this, lil' sister, smells like heaven came to roost.

"Before I begin my trek to pick up the kids, tell me what's going to happen tomorrow." I chew a piece of peeled carrot that somehow missed being thrown in with the other veggies.

"Glen suggests I take you to the Park and Ride tomorrow, then borrow your car for three appointments in Tacoma. He feels it's best to stay in Pierce County because it will draw less attention to your jury duty.

"The only problem I'm faced with," she says, "is that it's summer and the attorneys have vacation time off and that is going to draw things out—you know, a trial, hearing and such."

"You wanna come with me to pick up the kids?" I invite her.

"No, I need to finish dinner and set the table. I'm so glad there are things to keep my mind off my problems and my hands busy."

"The girls can set the table for you," I offer.

"We'll see, go … shoo … and hurry back, dinner's ready."

I decide as I pick up my car keys, *I'd love to bare my problems, but my sister has the weight of the world on her shoulders just now. Mine can wait. It's not knowing how much longer till Judge Daly finds out my deception that worries me. I wonder … Is it possible he already knows? Mary Alice did suggest at lunchtime that he acted stressed and we blamed it on Dr. Jarbouski. Could it be over me and he's waiting for me to come clean? Maybe it upset him because he knows how it will affect the outcome of the case? Mary Alice is right. He's afraid of tarnishing his image, of his olive leaf crown falling. It has nothing to do concerning Karin, who is a very sick gal.*

Chapter 9

Thursday, the sixth day of jury duty; I'm on the express headed for Seattle. The promise of a beautiful day, the mood around me is friendly. Every morning for the past week I've taken the bus with the same people. At first I understood they knew each other and I was the new kid on the block, but now they smile and even comment on the weather when I board.

Sleep contributes to my better disposition. Glen decided I shouldn't wait up for him. He let me know, "I'm quite capable of heating a plate of food or opening a can of soup." Bless him. I presume the man who crawled into my bed and turned out the light was my husband; I slept like the grateful dead the entire night.

The kids are restless, they've been on their best behavior but it's beginning to wear thin. Some of their antics are frustrating to me. I wish for the trial to end. We need to move ahead with summer plans. Maybe I'll get dropped from jury duty. *One day at a time,* I tell myself. *This too shall pass.*

Paula works the afternoon shift so the only information I get concerning her are notes Glen leaves, or hastily made phone calls during her lunch and coffee breaks. It doesn't give us much time for details. I know she's miserable; my heart goes out to her.

~ ~ ~

The trial commences with Judge Daly pompously ascending to his throne. Nice to see his brow isn't furrowed this morning.

The second witness for the defense is none other than Karin's mother, the woman I've observed sitting in the spectator gallery since the beginning of the trial. I thought she was a member of the Zen order. I would never have guessed her to be Karin's mother. And to think I felt sorry for Karin because none of her family attended the trial.

Mr. Dowd begins by introducing Mrs. Colby and has her tell us about herself. Still in shock over not recognizing her, I did catch that Mrs. Colby is secretary to the vice president of a chemical supply company in Seattle that manufactures industrial soaps and cleaners in a five-state region that includes Alaska and Hawaii.

In a tailored designer suit, she carries her slender build with dignity, her dark hair frames serious features; she portrays a most gracious lady but her stern controlled expression commands respect.

I can't help but notice how Karin glances at her now and again. Karin's relaxed attitude has vanished and is replaced by one, I'd like to say, of embarrassment.

Mr. Dowd asks Mrs. Colby to tell the court her knowledge of when her daughter's problems at home and school began.

Mrs. Colby requests a drink of water, then daintily sips before she dabs at her lips with a handkerchief. She goes on to describe her husband's hospitalization for mental illness.

"When Karin was around age three, my husband started getting obsessive about things I did. He was a difficult man to get along with. I was forced to work outside the home but tried to keep a clean house with meals on time. One day I came home late ... I worked late many times ... and found Lyle, my husband, curled up in a corner of the bedroom, crying like a baby.

"Karin was in her bedroom screaming. She hadn't been fed and she had wet her panties. I couldn't get Lyle to quiet down so I called the family doctor and he admitted my husband to a hospital where he stayed for around three or four months, I believe it was.

"We had used a young lady to baby sit Karin off and on when we went out to social functions. She came and stayed for a while but moved on and I was forced to hire nannies to care for Karin. Some were very ... some were all right."

Mrs. Colby straightened up in her chair and daintily patted her handkerchief across her face before continuing. "Life was pretty much routine for Karin until she left for college. Lyle was always in and out of hospitals. When he was home, he was useless; he couldn't do anything for himself, even less for Karin. He didn't function as a father.

"Because of my work, I'm away for long hours. I worked weeks without a day off. I was busy and didn't interview the nannies as I should have. I thought they were adequate; but now ... I'm not so sure." She paused as though in thought. "I don't know.

"Karin's a moody child. She's difficult to deal with. I wasn't even aware she wasn't managing her term at UW until after only one semester she told me she dropped out.

"I remember she came home and said she wanted to be a nurse. She said some of her teachers said she was compassionate and a caregiver. But you know... I didn't agree; she definitely wasn't sociable.

"At that time, I admit, I became upset; sounded to me like she was being flighty... avoiding work. Hard for me to understand; I've always worked hard and long hours, too.

"I gave her an ultimatum. 'You can live at home for six months but at the end of six months you're on your own.'"

Mrs. Colby admitted she wasn't at home during much of the six months. In fact, one time she'd accompanied her boss on a business trip to Europe.

"When I'm home, my relationship with Karin is uncomfortable and strained; as I stated before, Karin is moody and unsociable. She sulks a lot. I thought she was going through one of those phases ... you know, an attitude where the parent can't do anything right. She's always been negative toward my work—"

Mr. Dowd interrupted. "In what way was she negative?"

If Mr. Dowd was a doctor, I'd classify him as having poor bedside manners. However, I find Mrs. Colby is thoughtless. Why do I care how she's being treated?

"Oh … well …" Mrs. Colby's voice took on a stern tone. "I work for a chemical company. To Karin, I'm responsible for polluting the water. I destroy fish … birds."

"So," Mr. Dowd asked, "would you say most of your talks with Karin were argumentative?"

"Yes, when we did talk, it was always negative from her standpoint. We have nothing in common. Being with her drained my energy."

I remember going through this with my parents and I've sensed it in my children. There comes a point when it's difficult to hold a conversation with parents. Times change for parents. In this day and age, I make the same meaningful sacrifices with their best interest in mind. It's the parents' means of protecting their offspring. Our job, as parents and guardians, is to manage young lives. Instead, friendships between us don't necessarily develop into a bond but our obligations to each other turn to hostility.

I find I generalize that what I'm doing is for my kids' benefit. My husband takes a different approach; he retreats … 'I'll wait in the car; I'm going fishing; will get outta your hair.' It's like he doesn't want to be adviser or confidant; he doesn't want to spoil things for his kids.

Judge Daly's restless sigh attracts our attention, he confronts his watch while Mr. Dowd continues his interrogation.

"Well," Mrs. Colby said, "as to the ultimatum I mentioned earlier, at the end of six months, I asked Karin to show me her curriculum for the next semester. She admitted she hadn't done anything; she hadn't filled out a solitary form."

I feel bad for Karin. It hurts to hear that as a kid she was so alone. She ate alone, went to bed alone. She had no father to speak of and a working mother who did nothing with her daughter.

Mrs. Colby confesses, "It broke my heart; the girl was always slouching around. She didn't have friends. The nannies told me all she did, day after day, was eat, watch TV and sleep."

"Objection!" Mr. Clemens shouted out. "That's hearsay, Yer Honor."

Judge Daly confronts his watch for a second time before he answers, "Sustained. Mrs. Colby, please, just tell the court what you know to be fact."

"Your Honor," Mrs. Colby replied, "this is my only child, my daughter. I felt I had to take a firm hand with her; otherwise, Your Honor, she might never take responsibility for herself."

"Tell us, Mrs. Colby," Mr. Dowd slowly walked over to face the jury, "what did you do after Karin confessed she'd not applied for the nursing program?"

"I gave her some money and told her she was out of the house and on her own."

Not looking at the witness, Mr. Dowd asked, "Was that the last time you saw your daughter before her arrest this year?"

"No. She appeared ... probably a year or so later after I kicked her out. I came home from work one day and there she was. She looked like death warmed over. She was emaciated ... thin, pale. There was something obviously the matter with her. Her talk was slurred. I couldn't make out anything she said. She rambled something about Los Angeles and the Peace Corps program. I suspected she was on drugs and when I confronted her, she jumped up and stormed out of the house. That's the last I saw of her. I presumed she went back to California."

"Mrs. Colby, I realize my next question is a difficult one, but I think you will understand why I ask. Do you feel you did the right thing by sending your daughter away? Sending her off alone...on her own as you described the scene?"

Mrs. Colby paused before she answered. "Well sir, at the time I did the best I could," again she applied the handkerchief to her brow, "with the information I had then. But, knowing what I do now—yes, today I would do it differently."

"What makes you say that?"

We could see Mrs. Colby was uncomfortable. She had just admitted her mistake was calloused.

"When Karin quit college, I thought she was just being childish—her way to draw attention. I didn't see her do the things her fa ... Lyle did, so I didn't think of her as having mental problems.

"I thought setting rules and being firm with her would make her grow up. I didn't think of her as a mental case—not like her father." Mrs. Colby lowered her voice. "I couldn't bring myself to think that was possible." Her lowered head muffled her words. She wiped a hand hastily across her eyes before her head came up.

The jury watched Mrs. Colby straighten up and pull herself together. "I didn't want my daughter to become one of those spoiled, rich kids who become parasites to society. I thought if I practiced tough love with her... Now, I'm aware she had a problem, a mental problem and it's not her fault."

The sincerity in Mrs. Colby's voice sounds genuine. "I wish I'd known this before; I could have sent Karin to people who would have helped her."

Mr. Clemens voiced an immediate and loud objection. "This is all speculation, Yer Honor."

Judge Daly agreed.

Mr. Dowd next asked Mrs. Colby to read several marked passages from letters Karin sent her father while she was living at the Zen Foundation.

Mrs. Colby admits she never passed them on to Karin's father because she felt they would only serve to upset the man. "They were ramblings of an immature, sentimental, idiotic girl. They were about some kind of promises she made to herself that she would fulfill by herself by becoming enlightened ... that to fulfill her vow was 'to save all beings from suffering.'"

My impression, listening to the excerpts of the letters, was of how painfully insecure Karin was. She desperately needed or wanted to impress her father, but the words came out so pathetic and overly dramatic.

Judge Daly interrupted to announce, "We need a morning break and will resume Mrs. Colby's testimony when we return."

We stand at attention while Judge Daly gathers himself together and departs his throne. When he was no longer in view, we filed out of the room.

We, the jury, know we are not to discuss any of the proceedings, but I felt I had to let the others know how moved I am by the testimony thus far. I exhaled with an explosive, "Whew," followed by several agreements of, "Yeah!"

Settling down after the break, Mr. Dowd announced, "I have no further questions, Your Honor."

Addressing the prosecutor, Judge Daly asked, "Mr. Clemens, do you wish to cross-examine?"

I tried to concentrate and listen to the prosecutor's cross-examination of Karin's mother but with little success.

Thoughts of my sister and her family, Mr. Clemens' gentle voice and Mrs. Colby's subdued responses faded in and out of my attention.

I wonder, *Will this same scene be repeated for Paula and Mark? Their children are involved and though Glen and I may be awarded their guardianship, what will eventually happen to them?*

There seems little the professionals take as responsibility for Mark's grave illness; he's mentally sick and there seems to be little interest in his condition outside of giving him relaxation drugs and sending him home.

Suddenly, the interrogation turned ugly. Mr. Clemens asked Mrs. Colby when she began to believe that mental illness was the cause of Karin's problems and her violent behavior at the Zen church."

Mrs. Colby's expression is of undisguised disgust; she glared at Mr. Clemens. "You ask me when did I think Karin became mentally sick? Isn't it obvious? Let me tell you … a sane woman doesn't do what Karin did … a sane person doesn't act that way. When I heard what happened … it was obvious she wasn't sane. Look at her." Mrs. Colby stares in Karin's direction. "Look at her … you can tell by looking at her she hasn't the least idea what's going on. She's on trial for murder and look at her sitting there like she's watching some TV show. Oh spare me the insinuation I've not been a good mother."

As suddenly as Mrs. Colby erupted, she calmed. "I'm sorry for my conduct. I want you to know, I tried to hire a private lawyer to handle this—not some unknown public defender, but Karin wouldn't … what the hell does Karin know?"

The prosecutor stopped Mrs. Colby with a held up hand. "Ah move that last comment be stricken from the record. That statement insults ma colleague, Mr. Dowd. Mrs. Colby, yer statement is most uncalled for."

At first, I thought, *It's so like Mr. Clemens to be so chivalrous but then it occurred to me, of course, Karin wouldn't let her mother hire a more experienced lawyer. Mr. Clemens, the sly ole man, is supporting the defense attorney's claim that Karin is not thinking clearly.*

Mr. Clemens addressed the court recorder. "Would ya be so kind as ta please … go back and read the part of Mrs. Colby's testimony where she mentions her daughter using drugs?"

We listened to the excerpts read from the record. Mr. Clemens then asked, "Do ya, Mrs. Colby, think … is it possible the drugs had any effect on yer daughter? And isn't it possible, Mrs. Colby, these same drugs affected yer daughter's mind?"

"Objection, Your Honor," Mr. Dowd protested. "The blood tests taken just after the incident show Karin was not using drugs at the time of the retreat. And furthermore, the witness is not an expert on drugs. I object … there is no foundation for this line of questioning."

With the charm of a cultured southern gentleman, Mr. Clemens shot back, "Just because the drugs weren't in her blood stream that day doesn't mean … that is, Ah guess what Ah'm tryin' ta say is … couldn't the drugs have already affected her mind in some way? Isn't it possible?"

Judge Daly agreed with Mr. Clemens and overruled the objection.

Mrs. Colby said she wasn't a doctor, she couldn't possibly say when the drugs and mental illness began. "But I know one thing," blurted Mrs. Colby, pointing directly at Mr. Clemens, "She was having mental problems long before she got near any of those drugs. You're trying to make an argument that my daughter couldn't have been sick because if I were a normal parent, especially one with a sick husband, I would have noted similarities. Yes, well maybe I should have caught on to Karin's problem a lot earlier.

"You know something, Mr. Prosecutor, the reason I didn't catch on to Karin's condition was because the problem wasn't there. Insinuate I'm not a normal parent, all right. I failed as a mother, all right. I failed my daughter. There … is that what you want me to say?"

We, the jury, viewed Mrs. Colby, a shaken woman. Her confession came as a deeply embarrassing admittance of guilt from a proud woman. Tears melted her mascara and coursed a path through her makeup, but she held her head up with dignity.

I find her an unlikable woman, but she has been loyal to her husband through his years of mental illness, and she is willing, by her admission of being a poor mother, to accept the responsibility for what has happened to Karin.

I had to stop listening. I was shaken by the exchange between Mr. Clemens and Mrs. Colby. I felt caught in my own family situation.

I couldn't bear to hear anymore of the testimony and handle my problems.

Mary Alice reached across Mike and punched me out of my reverie. "Come on," she whispered, "stand up; *Royal Big Bird* wants to fly the coop."

I stood up and suddenly I was bone tired … tired of trying to decide the fate of Karin and her problems, tired of my own situation and circumstances. How much longer could I play out my little charade?

CHAPTER 10

Once home, before I pressure cook a chicken to go along with potatoes and cabbage mash, I'll collect my children from their various sports obligations. The hungry boys ask, "What's for supper?" Then order dumplings along with the chicken. In approximately two hours after climbing from the bus, my family sits down to dinner.

Homework finished, the dishwasher going, I join the family to watch *Mod-Squad* when the telephone rings.

Ten-year-old Jake, closest to the phone, pulled himself up off the floor without missing a scene on TV. He answered then extended the phone to me—"Mom?"

I inquire, "Who is it?"

"I dunno, think it's Aunt Paula."

"I'll take it in the kitchen." I race for the wall phone. "Hi, sis."

Paula responds. "Hi, Jo. Got gobs to tell you; are you free to talk?"

"How come you're calling at this hour? Oh … day off, huh? What's new?" The phone held to my ear I manage with one toe to pull out a chair from under the table.

"I finally got through to our public defender; he said the judge set bail. I saw Mark for a bit yesterday. It isn't easy walking away when I know how confused and miserable he is."

"What did he have to say?"

"He's pretty hurt that he was arrested like a criminal in front of Tammy. He said he told the cops he didn't feel what they did was right. There had to be a better way. He said they came for him with guns, batons and pepper spray in front of the kids.

"Mark said he did as he was told. He placed his hands on the kitchen counter and spread his legs, while a cop patted him down in all the right places and a few others. He said the one cop acted halfway human when he told him to turn around and put his hands behind him.

"Mark said he told the cop, 'You don't need handcuffs, I'm not running anywhere, especially with my kids here.' He said another cop yelled at him 'shut up and hold still.'

"He had his rights read to him and waited until the cop was through to ask what they intended for him to do about his children, or were the kids going with him?

"He said, 'One of the officers said he'd handle it and made a phone call.' Mark said he told them to call his wife, but they were in such a hurry to get him out of the house a couple of the officers said they'd stay with the kids until a CPS worker arrived.

"He remembers someone saying, 'We aren't allowed to take the kids anywhere until someone comes up with documents from the court making them wards of the state.'

"Mark said, 'The cops were nervous about having to waste time waiting for legal permission to remove Tammy and Jeff from the premises. But they wouldn't hear of me staying with my very own kids till someone came.'

"According to Mark, it was bedlam. Tammy was screaming and crying and at the same time an officer asked if he understood his rights read to him. He overheard an officer say, 'Rape of a child is a first degree offense.'

"Mark said it embarrassed him to see the neighbors who gathered at the door when they saw the cops come. I guess he got pretty upset when one of them asked, 'What's he done?' And one of the policemen said, 'Rape.'

JR Reynolds

"Mark said he yelled, 'I didn't rape anyone.' He told me he didn't recognize the man who asked, 'What child?'

"When they got him downtown, Mark said he was led into a small room with a wooden table and chairs where they removed his handcuffs. On the way to the room he noticed a number of offices occupied by policemen in gray-blue uniforms equipped with black guns, black holsters and black sticks. Just like in a crime movie.

"After what seemed hours to Mark, he said he thought they'd forgotten him. A policeman finally showed up and took him out of the room long enough to book, fingerprint and photograph him, then put him back in the same room.

"He told me he sat for hours. No coffee, no cigarettes, no water, no food, not even a restroom; I'm surprised he could laugh when he told me, 'Not even a radio.'

"He said it was pathetic. 'They say I committed a crime so I'm being punished. I always said, bad deeds will come back to haunt you.'

"Jo, I think he believes for what happened in Vietnam he's being punished.

"He ... he says he's had time to analyze between being alone and lonely. He can handle being alone, it's natural, but lonely is something that exists in the mind and it's like a virus; it has to survive in a host. When he thinks about the position he's in, he feels lonely, like he alone has to fight off depression and not give in to despair."

I swallow past a lump in my throat hearing this. "So what's he waiting for if the judge set bail? Why's he still there?"

"He was waiting for a public defender."

"Didn't you call for one? I thought that was one of the first things you did, Paula."

"I did, Jo, but they're busy people and we had to wait our turn. Mark is being held at the jail in Tacoma, but I haven't told you everything. Listen to this.

"His defender did show up this morning; this is Mark's description of him. 'A big, boisterous, bold, brash, brazen, bullish, bellowing man.' Mark said he rushed the desk and blasted the cops on duty after learning Mark hadn't had his meds and went ballistic as to why bail hadn't been posted."

- 80 -

"Paula, I thought you delivered Mark's medications. How does Mark know all this?"

"The cops told him they found the medications in with his other personal effects. Someone forgot to pass them along. I told you I was with Mark for a bit yesterday.

"Jo, listen to the rest of this; this monstrous, big burley sumo wrestler, introduced himself as Mr. Dennis. Mark said he doesn't speak but bellows, and said, 'What the …. is this all about, Mr. Markham?' Jo, I'm not repeating the four letter word. And when Mark said it was nothing, Mr. Dennis yelled so loud the entire precinct, including those walking past outside, had to have heard him. The little four letter word again. 'The …. it isn't, Mark,' Mr. Dennis yelled. 'The hum dee dum dum it's … it's nothing to you?'

"Mark said he told him, 'She's lying, Mr. Dennis, the girl's lying.'

"Mark said Dennis yelled, 'Is she? Did you have intercourse with this girl? The guy hollers like I'm deaf.'

"Mark answered, 'No!'

"Then Mr. Dennis yelled, 'Did you penetrate any of her orifices with your genitals or any other object?'

"Mark said he just stared at Mr. Dennis. It was obvious the man didn't believe him. So he told me, he refused to answer.

"I guess after Mark wouldn't talk to him, Mr. Dennis said for Mark's benefit, 'I can't figure why a fifteen-year-old girl would file bogus charges against you.'

"Mark said he didn't say a thing but told me, 'When I refused to talk to the idiot, Mr. Dennis got red in the face, wheezed, pointed his fat sausage finger at me and demanded to know, 'Do these terms fit anywhere in the concept of your interest? … *Pedophile, sex offender, statutory rapist, child molester?'*

"Mark said he didn't say a word but watched Mr. Dennis grind his teeth until the muscles in his jaw bulged. Finally he told Mark, 'I'll be in my office till eight-thirty this evening. Don't keep me late.'

"Mark told me he did a slow burn and stated as calmly as possible to Mr. Dennis, 'I'm not guilty but no one believes me. Any records will show I'm a law-abiding citizen that just spent two years in Nam, if that means anything. And I've two kids of my own.'

"Anyway," Paula conveyed further, "before Mr. Dennis left the room, I guess Mark asked him, 'Where's my kids? Mr. Dennis, I've not been accused in a court of law of being guilty to anything. I didn't do anything. Soon as I'm out of here, I'm gonna get my kids. They're innocent. Why punish them?'

"Mark said Mr. Dennis nearly bit his head off. 'Don't!' he snapped. 'Let them be. Now is not the time. You're stuck in quicksand, Mark. You don't struggle when you're in quicksand.'

"Mark told me," I heard Paula catch her breath, "he felt himself beginning to crumble and said, 'So, not only do you accuse me of being guilty but now I'm buried in quicksand. Is that it, Mr. Dennis?'

"And Dennis's reply was, 'Mark, you're in the most quickest possible sand right now. And don't even think about leaving the state.'"

I asked, "So then what happened?"

"Mark said, 'Mr. Dennis turned and started out the door, then bellowed over his shoulder at me ... and for chrissake, Mark, don't even *look* at another fifteen-year-old girl.'"

"I'm confused. So is Mark out of jail?"

"He's on his way to the VA Hospital in Seattle. He's been without his meds. Jo. I'm scared ... I know he's dehydrated, sleep deprived, and he tries but he can't hide his pain from me. How can you have diarrhea when you haven't eaten for three days?"

I want to tell Paula that Mark might be psychotic, but I don't dare. Karin Colby's case isn't like Mark's mental illness. But again, when I listened to the witnesses speak in Karin's behalf, I recognize similarities.

"So, sis," I ask Paula, "where do we go from here?"

"I'm familiar with his routine at the VA Hospital. I'll wait till Mark calls before I pick him up. Thank God the kids are safe. I know they have to be suffering separation anxiety but I tell myself they're in good hands. I just don't know about getting them home ... what I have to do.

"Oh, Jo," Paula sighs, then asks, "By the way, how's jury duty coming along?"

"I live one day at a time," I reply. "On one hand, I'm waiting to be thrown off the case. There just might be two jailbirds in the family. On the other hand, I'll ride out the trial. Can't tell you anything; I'm not supposed to discuss the case, remember?"

"You're feeling guilty because of Mark, aren't you?" Paula asks. "I wish the courts here didn't have to find out about Mark's mental condition. Jo, they can blow it all out of proportion. What do you think?"

"I'd like to strangle that Kathy; she's a little witch, in my opinion."

"Mine too," Paula stated. "I inquired how best to contact Kathy or her family when I visited Mark yesterday. Like what kind of documentation would I need if they were to talk to me?

"The woman at the desk, I presume she was a cop, said not to make waves right now ... wait and ask my attorney. She wouldn't advise contact ... wasn't an option."

"You know, Paula, if I get to finish this case, I'll learn how the courts work. I might be able to ... no, forget it ... forget I said anything. 'Strike it from the record,' is how they say it in court."

"No. Tell me, Jo, what were you going to say? We've always confided in each other, tell me."

"Paula, I've got to get up early; don't forget to say your prayers. Remember ... Mom always told us to 'Take it to the Lord in prayer.'"

"Jo, that's from a hymn," Paula giggled.

"Oh, is it? Well, Mom's intentions were always meant for our good. Maybe someone wrote the hymn after they heard her say it. I was her favorite you know? Remember? She said she wore out her knees praying for me. I had to be pretty special if she was that thankful."

"Well then," Paula purred, "you shouldn't have any problems. Are you saying, if we bend our knees, God will take over? Is that what you're saying? You're not that naïve, Jo. Give me a break."

"Now now, Paula, remember Mama and look where it got her. She's probably right this minute playing that harp she always wanted."

"Yeah, I hear you. But, Jo, not everyone is a Quaker like Mama."

"I didn't know that? But life was the same for her as for us, dear sister. We have to keep our faith, Paula, we have to keep our faith. For me, it's I hope I don't get thrown in jail with Mark. Incidentally, I think his defense attorney sounds great. Think I might need him. I'll keep Mr. Dennis's name in mind."

When at last I fell into bed, I thought of my conversation with Paula and felt better about their situation. *It's going to be a rough road ahead for her. Especially after the witnesses I've listened to and don't understand. Mark's best bet is to rely on his court appointed defense to convince the jury of his innocence.*

Take me ... one minute I'm sure Karin's guilty but the next I feel she doesn't know what's happening in the world around her. I'm thoroughly confused. Neither Karin or Mark are guilty until proven guilty.

Mortals are what we are ... just mortals ... until we walk in Karin or Mark's shoes, or follow in their footsteps. How can we possibly see the world as they view it? As they live it?

Those without sin, cast the first stone. Judge not lest you be judged. My God, as I know him, is not a vengeful God. Then, I wonder, why are we so rough on each other?

CHAPTER 11

Friday, the seventh day of my jury duty. The court does not hear new cases on Fridays. The courthouse I enter today is quiet without the hustle of daily business.

I slip into my seat just before the bailiff closes the courtroom door to signify the beginning of our day. Mary Alice and I exchange quick nods as she mouths, "Mornin'."

From his throne, I sense his Royal Highness, Judge Daly staring straight at me. *Oh-oh,* my heart skips a beat; *bet he's found out my circumstances and I'm headed outta here … fast as he can boot me.*

"Ladies and gentlemen of the jury," Judge Daly begins. *Here it comes; will he ostracize me before everyone?*

He continues, "We'll resume the testimony for the State versus Karin Colby this morning. It's Friday and I know you're all looking forward to the long weekend ahead, so let's get on with the questioning. If you will, Mr. Dowd."

Mr. Dowd requests an emaciated appearing little woman with short hair to take the witness stand. Our attention is at once drawn to a loud whispering commotion from the Japanese group in the gallery; they abruptly stand up and together vacate the room. Their disturbance did not go unnoticed.

The witness's name is Phyllis Delacroix. She is a historian and has interest in the Zen Foundation for professional reasons. Her college professor recommended she become involved with the Zen practice when she showed interest in Japanese history and their profound concentration customs.

She joined the Zen order in Kirkland and discovered after a few years she had developed more than an interest in the practice of meditation so she moved in and devoted all her energy to practicing meditation full-time.

Karin shifting noisily in her chair catches my attention. She refrains from looking at Miss Delacroix; in fact, she's restless and appears tense for some reason.

Mr. Dowd inquired, "Miss Delacroix, would you describe your impression of Karin from the first day you met her?"

Her hands folded in her lap, she sits in the same rigid posture as the first witness, the Buddhist monk. "The very first day Karin walked in," she said, "I could tell there was something wrong with her. She needed a therapist, not a Zen Master. Zen lessons were a waste of time on her."

Karin broke into loud laughter—the first noise out of her since the trial began and came as a surprise to everyone.

As though unaware of Karin, the witness continues, "I remember at the house meeting, we had to decide whether to let her become a resident and I was against it. From the very beginning I knew something was wrong with her."

Mr. Dowd asks, "Did you express your concern?"

"Sure ... I said, 'We don't run a halfway house for lonely women. This is a Zen center.' I knew it would be a problem to have her there because she was obviously a mixed-up troublemaker. But I got voted down; you know how it is?"

Miss Delacroix explains she no longer lives at the Zen Foundation Center. "I left right after the murder. I'd been planning to leave for some time, anyway."

Mr. Dowd urges her to disclose the reason for her decision.

"Because ... I disagree with the late Zen Master's teaching technique. He put way too much pressure on his students to achieve *enlightenment*.

"Mr. Nishimura was always saying, 'If you're serious about Zen, then you have to really push yourself. It brings about a sudden enlightenment and it will be the greatest experience of your life.' He actually said you had to practically kill yourself if you wanted to attain the goal.'"

She pauses, swallows, then moistens her lips with her tongue. "I got tired of her attitude. It's downright snobbish to my way of thinking. My opinion is that Mr. Nishimura thinks since he had to go through hell to get his knowledge, you're expected to follow and go through hell too or you're not good enough to join the cult.

"Then when you get someone like Karin who's already on the edge and becomes possessed … you know what I mean? … You have to agree, I'm right. Look at what happened if you don't believe me."

"So you feel that Mr. Nishimura's—" Mr. Dowd attempted to rephrase her words. "In your opinion, his teaching method is what pushed Miss Colby over the edge during the retreat?"

The witness twists her face and mouth up to one side as her gaze wanders around the room. "Well, not intentionally," she pauses. "But I do think the koan he assigned to Karin, the one about killing the Buddha in the road. I'll always contend it had something to do with it … yeah … you're right. I guess you best described it correctly."

Mr. Dowd, on the way to his table, indicates to Judge Daly he has no further questions for the witness.

Mr. Clemens rises slowly to deliver his direct examination. In his polite, southern, cynical manner, he reports, "A prior witness mentioned in a statement that Karin had been quite upset … as were many of the Zen Foundation members … concernin' romantic relationships that existed between the late Zen teacher and several female members of his church, including our present witness."

Mr. Clemens looks straight at the jury and clears his throat. "The reason you saw Mr. Nishimura's relatives leave the courtroom is … and it's interestin' ta note … one of the romantically involved females from the church brought a sexual harassment suit against Mr. Nishimura. It was settled out of court but not before it became of interest ta the public."

It surprises me that Miss Delacroix didn't seem taken aback when exposed during his statement. I wonder, *Maybe the prosecuting attorney and she are friends?*

Miss Delacroix admits to us, the jury, "Yes, the scandal did upset a lot of people, including Karin."

She told of one night when a woman member accused Mr. Nishimura of being a fraud and someone else suggested he be thrown out of the foundation and another member said he shouldn't be allowed to teach.

She added, "That was the night Karin didn't yell at anyone but ran off to her room and later several of the members said they heard her crying. But then ... there'd been a lot of crying going on at that time."

"Tell us, Miz Delacroix, so's we understand clearly," Mr. Clemens requests in his charming drawl. "Before this incident came out in the open ... open for the public that is, did ya'll have any reason ta think Karin liked Mr. Nishimura? Ah mean ... maybe had a bit of a crush on him?"

This man impresses me, how he manages to be kind, even while he's asking the most intrusive questions.

At Mr. Clemens' suggestion, Karin again burst into loud rancorous laughter. We jurors watch her shake her head vigorously.

"No, I don't believe she gave me any reason to think so," Miss Delacroix replies. "In fact, Karin knew the rules concerning a *bhikkhuni* (Buddhist nun). She never talked to me about her feelings. In fact she never looked me in the eye and practically ran the other way whenever I was near her."

I watch Mr. Clemens nod slowly. Then I glance at Karin and note she is nonchalantly inspecting her fingernails on one hand, a frown covers her face.

What if, I imagine. *What if our immature Karin had a crush on the Zen Master and found him sleeping with Miss Delacroix?... Oh dear God. Could it be ... perhaps... the murder was planned after all?*

Mr. Clemens thanks the witness and advises Judge Daly he's finished with his cross-examination. We jurors are astounded ... in shock.

Judge Daly calls for a fifteen minute break. After he departs the room, the bailiff holds open the gate of the jury gallery for us to file out.

Mary Alice corners me. "I was afraid you weren't going to make it this morning. How come you look so beat? I mean I have bags under my eyes but you're carrying suitcases."

"Just a lot on my mind," I confess. "I don't know about your house but my kids are beginning to rebel. School's out in a few weeks and then what? We made vacation plans but everything's up in the air."

And, I don't dare tell you about my sister Paula and her Mark and the worry I carry around of being found out that I lied to get on jury duty.

"After this morning," Mary Alice comments as Mike walks up.

"After this morning, what?" he questions loudly.

"After this morning, I hope the day goes fast," Mary Alice quickly ad-libs.

"Yeah, sure is slow ain't it?" Mike agrees. "Whoopee! I get to sleep in tomorrow. It's gonna feel good, let me tell you. Got tickets for me and ma kids to take in a Rainiers' home game tomorrow night. Know what ya mean about gettin' the day over with." He rubs his palms together vigorously. "Got places to go and things to do."

"We better get back," prompts Mary Alice, guiding us towards the courtroom.

Mr. Dowd's next witness is a Professor Stephen Griswold, who teaches a course in comparative religion at Bellevue Community College. My guess, looking at him, this poor miserable man has health issues.

He details his testimony with his philosophy that the Zen sect of Buddhism encourages impulsive, spontaneous behavior. He advocates, "Zen teaches everything as an illusion and that all value judgments like good or wrong are meaningless.

"Zen has no concept of sin, that's all in your mind. If you do something bad, then it's bad. You've created bad *karma,* which I understand to mean, painful memories that are destined to plague you forever. However ... if you do something wrong without knowing it was wrong, then it's not bad karma. You don't suffer regrets that follow you around the rest of your life."

"So," Mr. Dowd inquires, with a show of gusto, "according to Zen, you can do anything and get away with it as long as you think it's okay? Is that what you're saying? Murder, if it's done with a clear mind, is not wrong?"

"Right." The professor rubs at his swollen, red-rimmed eyes with one hand. "If you look at the samurais, a warrior class in old Japan, they had this *ideal* of being able to go into battle, or even to kill themselves, without any doubts or fears. This practice in recent times is demonstrated by the kamikaze pilots during the Second World War. They were students of the Zen philosophy that taught them to calm their minds before their suicidal attacks."

Mr. Dowd nods his approval then turns to us. "That leads to my last question, Professor. That puzzle about killing the Buddha in the road … are you familiar with it?"

"Yes, I've heard of it."

"Can you, sir, tell us what it means?"

Professor Griswold frantically fumbles for his handkerchief in time to cover his mouth as he gives into a fit of coughing. After gaining control of himself he uncovers his mouth and wipes his nose.

"I'm sorry. Yes … the koan about killing a Buddha. Zen philosophers would like to insist that you can't explain koans in words, but I believe that the general idea is that even if the Buddha himself appears in front of you, their theory is you ought to be able to cut him down without a second thought. It would be the extreme test of your calm state of mind."

In a strangled nasal voice, Professor Griswold explains, "You understand …like regular Buddhism, Zen places a lot of emphasis on detachment."

I wonder; *Is it just me or do the others feel this detachment is like some type of anesthesia. It's like taking some kind of pain killer that gives you that feeling of being detached. Why would you want to be detached or without control of yourself?*

In other words, are you alive? The professor gives me the impression Zen is an excruciatingly slow psychological suicide.

Zen doesn't recognize any moral code either. Did Karin attain her enlightenment? So, am I to understand that killing the Zen Master didn't go against any principles of their religion? So why are we here?

Mr. Dowd's next statement answers my questions. He explains why he called this witness. "To show," he says to us, "how vigorously amoral and bizarre the Zen cult is." He also states, "It's a two—edged sword, because it raises the question: What if Karin is just a good Zen student?"

Mr. Dowd turns to the witness. "Professor Griswold, then you agree that Karin's psychological problems are valuable assets of the Zen church that helped push her toward an 'enlightenment'?"

"I do—yes."

Mr. Dowd states he has no further questions.

Excusing the witness, Judge Daly announces, "Court will adjourn until one o'clock."

An instant afterthought causes Mr. Dowd to turn and impulsively inquire, "Then would Miss Colby have been considered a great *shang* if she'd been a male living in Japan, say … two … three hundred years ago?"

I glance up to see Judge Daly's bushy eyebrows lift then quickly settle. Preparing to leave, he remains silent.

"Do you want me to answer that?" The professor looks perplexed. But he's already been excused.

Gathering his *wings* … excuse me … his robe sleeves, Judge Daly departs the room. *Hail, mighty Daly, King Daly*. But he hurries for his chamber before I can bend from the waist and sweep the floor with my hand.

I follow Mary Alice and fellow jurist Mrs. Judson out into the bright afternoon sunshine. "Beautiful," breathes Mary Alice.

"Yes, rather a pleasant day, isn't it?" Laura Judson agrees.

The benches are full so we find a grassy spot on the lawn and lower ourselves down. We have yet to open our lunches when Laura wrinkles her nose, forms her mouth into a small moue and fans the air. "What a dreadful, nasty odor; where's it coming from?"

"It's urine; someone's peed here," Mary Alice volunteers and quickly pushes herself up. "I'm going back inside."

"You know," I said, following the other two, "it makes sense; these homeless … where's the nearest restroom at night? Aren't they allowed to sleep on the lawn at night?"

"I'm sure I don't know." Laura brushes off her trim skirt and heads for the door. "I certainly can't eat my lunch out here."

"We'll be lucky to find a seat indoors," Mary Alice warns, "and we're sure to run into Mike."

"I'll take my chances." I hurry to catch up. "I can't believe that smell and why isn't the grass brown if it's been peed on?"

We find an empty bench at the far end of the hall and plunk ourselves down for the remainder of the lunch hour. Our small talk safely turns to books we enjoy. Laura's intrigued with Michener's *Hawaii,* which

Mary Alice finds too big. "A thick book," she sighs, "I recently put it aside for lighter reading."

Our lunch hour ends without Mike infringing on us, but before we enter the courtroom, there he is holding the door. "Be glad when this is over," he grumbles, "I'm gettin' burned with all this psychology jazz; how much longer they gonna bore us to death?"

"Oh, don't be such a cynic, Mike," I criticize.

The other two shush Mike. "You're gonna get us in trouble, Mike," Laura warns him in as loud a whisper as she dares. The other jurors glare at Mike as they push past him for their seats.

"Kill me with a stick, if ya will," Mike hisses on the way to his seat.

Judge Daly already seated gives the impression he's been waiting for us, just as Mike's whisper, "This show is gettin' damn old," carries throughout the courtroom.

If heard by Judge Daly, he doesn't blink an eye, but inquires, "Mr. Clemens, are you ready? Begin, if you please."

"Professor Griswold, is it?" Mr. Clemens ambles across the room to the witness stand. "You already told the court your academic qualifications, so Ah'm not gonna take up the court's time ... but Ah do need ta clarify a few details, sir.

"Now, first of all, Professor Griswold, ya call yerself professor, do ya not? Yes. Well, sir, for the record, isn't it a fact that yer basic academic degree is in theology rather than comparative religion?"

Before Professor Griswold can utter a word, Mr. Clemens continues, "And so, ta hep me understand here, Professor Griswold ... what Ah need ta understand is where did ya come by yer knowledge of Asian religion? ... Wasn't it from independent research and readin'?"

"Yes, some of it—"

Mr. Clemens quickly interrupts, "Didn't the college accept yer qualifications ta teach *only* an introductory course called *Religions of the World*?"

"Yes."

"And isn't it true, Professor, that ya devoted only one week of a six-week course ta all of Buddhism ... includin' Zen?"

"Yes."

I'm stunned. *Is Mr. Clemens calling the professor a fake, a fraud, and a charlatan?*

Mr. Clemens, just as quickly as he made reference to the professor's credentials, softened his undermining of the professor's testimony by inquiring about concerns relating to Christianity that allows the professor to give only yes and no answers.

"In yer biblical translation, Professor Griswold, isn't it true there are some churches perform services where believers are invited ta eat the flesh and drink the blood of their God?"

"Yes, sir."

"And doesn't," Mr. Clemens inquires, "the Bible tell us that God allowed Job ta be punished by Satan? Ah fail ta understand the logic. That he took from him all he loved dearly, his family … he lost everythin'. And later, everythin' was replaced with more than Job owned before … but what about his first family? It means little ta God that Job might have loved his first family and God merely replaced them with others and expected Job ta be satisfied?"

"Well…Yes."

"Ah never understood this, Professor. And, sir, didn't Christ once say, 'Ah came into this world ta set a man against his father, the daughter against her mother and the daughter-in-law against her mother-in-law? Does yer Good Book read like mine, Professor?"

The professor, suddenly possessed with a fit of coughing, can only shake his head. Before fully recovered, in a nasal sounding voice, he exclaims, "You've taken those quotations out of context, sir."

Mr. Clemens apologizes and admits he did. "It's not ma intention ta insult Christianity or the witness. But, Professor Griswold, with due respect, sir, Ah find yer testimony … that it has the same defects.

"Let me clarify myself, sir, if ya will?" Mr. Clemens leans on the witness rail. "The point ya made earlier that the kamikaze pilots used Zen ta prepare for battle …" Mr. Clemens first scratches his head then brushes his hair with the flat of his hand. "Ah believe … was it not yer point, sir? Yes … Ah believe you intended ta show us that … this is what takes place when people practice Zen, is it not?

"Need Ah remind ya, Professor, that Christianity was abused in precisely the same way durin' the Great Crusades and Inquisition? What does this tell us about Christianity? Therefore, with due respect, Professor, Ah classify you not as a specialist in the field of comparative religion but as a specialist in Christian theology, would this not be correct, sir?"

Mr. Clemens is an astute gentleman, his southern charisma only grows stronger as the trial proceeds. His age, his unkempt appearance, his middle-aged paunch and his gracious southern manners give him a parental style that I find impressive.

Mr. Dowd, on the other hand, is too fresh and rough. I find myself wondering after he's made a sensible summation, if he's not trying to manipulate us. His technique just doesn't come across as sincere.

Judge Daly ends our day after Mr. Clemens states, "No further questions, Yer Honor."

I feel as Mike said earlier, "Whoopee!" I'm free, weary and exhausted, but free. I bid the others a good weekend and head for the express and home to my other world.

Chapter 12

After a busy holiday weekend, I'm on the bus heading into Seattle. It's Tuesday morning, eighth day of the Karin Colby murder trial.

As the express races along, my mind replays Monday, Memorial Day. We invited friends, who were still in town, to share a potluck supper. Our foster sons had visitations with their parents.

It was a solemn occasion for two reasons: First, our family visited the Military Cemetery to pay our respects to the fallen soldiers. It's an emotional experience to observe the tiny American flags rippling in a breeze at the head of white identical markers that commemorate row upon row of those who lost their lives to preserve our freedoms.

The second reason, Mark and Paula with their family aren't with us this year. Mark isn't allowed around the children, so Paula traded days with another co-worker with a family.

Our neighbors, Vic and Deedee, attended the picnic with Vic's Great-Uncle Hugh. "He'll talk your leg off, if you let him," Vic whispers a warning to Glen and me.

It's from Uncle Hugh, I learn of another case of injustice, so relevant to our weak legal system.

Uncle Hugh went into great lengths to tell us how, when he was a young lad, his brothers served in World War One. "I remember their return home from the Great War."

He settled back in his lawn chair, still agile for his age, and removed the cap from a Heidelberg I offer. "This day," he said, "sure brings to mind alotta memories of back then.

"The fellas got home," he began with little prompting, "and were promised by Mr. Hoover, President of the United States, that the bonus certificates they got for service rendered was good as cash. But in the meantime, Mr. Hoover changed his mind about usin' treasury funds to pay bonus checks. So he puts 'em in a fund fer the fellas when they was to retire. They never got a red cent ... not one plug nickel.

"Now ma folks were havin' a hard time as 'twas, so the boys up and went to find work. When they came home now and again, they told us horror stories of what happened to 'em.

"Like I 'member this one time, my oldest brother Lamont told how he lived in a hobo camp, ya see? He told us, 'The people lived in anything they could find ... tents, chicken coops, shacks made of cardboard, fruit crates, and tar paper; that 'twas till they'se destroyed in about an hour's time. These families tried to live normal lives; they planted gardens, raised their families; they shared with each other as much as they was able.'

Uncle Hugh held us spellbound.

"Anyways, my brother said, 'The people, fed up with how the government was treatin' 'em, protested and when Vice President, Mr. Curtis, heard about the camp, he called out the cavalry who rode through the camp on horseback, destroyin' the gardens and homes. They used sabers and guns to shoot and kill people, many of 'em was veterans.'

"Ma brother told ma folks, 'We were the men who fought tooth and limb in Argonne, France and they run us over like dogs.'"

My son interrupted, "But didn't the police try to stop the cavalry?"

"Son," Uncle Hugh paused, "Mr. Curtis was Vice President; he didn't even have the jurisdiction to call in the militia as he did and by the time Mr. Hoover heard about it and sent General MacArthur with a troop, 'twas too late."

Vic prompted Uncle Hugh. "Tell how the newspapers handled it."

"Why, they wrote a story about how the veterans used their money already and was protestin' for more and President Hoover was quoted as sayin', 'He applauded MacArthur for sparin' the public treasury. The nation was bein' bled dry by veterans, like these men, who offend our common decency. Little justice back then, I tell ya."

Listening intently with furrowed brow, our son asked, "But wasn't that a lie? The newspapers saying they were criminals."

"Yep," Uncle Hugh nodded. "They was treated like criminals. Newspapers say whatever they want to say, son, you can't believe everything in print."

I was relieved when my kids complained they were hungry and Glen jumped up to grill the hamburgers.

Again, I asked myself, *where was the justice for these men who fought for America? Justice for all, we say, but is this true or do we simply pay lip service, recite a rote phrase with little meaning?*

~ ~ ~

I enter a silent courtroom late. The other jurors are already seated. I immediately lapse into thought of last Friday night; *Glen had taped a note to the fridge. 'Will call during my lunch hour. Be home.'*

Glen's call wasn't good news. Child Protective Services called to report that we are unqualified to take our niece and nephew, Tammy and Jeff. CPS is looking into finding a foster home for them. Mr. and Mrs. Steve is a receiving home and CPS feels they need to free the home for incoming emergency cases.

I had a suspicion this would happen. Glen and I know about receiving homes. When we first applied to take foster children, it was suggested we be a receiving home. The children are not screened, they come straight from harrowing, traumatic situations into a receiving home. Our children are already required to adapt and sacrifice for the needs of foster brothers. New first time children require special attention.

It hurts to be told we, as relatives, are not acceptable to take our own flesh and blood; however, CPS is correct. Under the circumstances, children removed from their existing homes are fragile and it's the responsibility of Child Protective Services to put them into a protective environment.

My Saturday morning was already a nightmare with so many details but whenever Paula calls, I give her my undivided attention. She is near tears. "Yesterday the court ruled the only visitation allowed for Mark to see the kids must be under supervision of a caseworker."

I'm proud of Paula keeping a stiff upper lip.

"He has no rights, Jo, and he's not been proven guilty. What's fair about our legal system that condemns a man before he's had a fair trial?"

"So?" I asked Paula, "What does your counselor have to say?"

"Jo, these public defender guys are tied up for months. There is nothing we can do but play their waiting game. Mark can't leave the state, he can't be seen in a bar, can't be around other kids, even yours. We can't come around you for any reason. If he does and is found out, he could be thrown right back in jail and wait out his time till a trial date has been set."

~ ~ ~

Why is Judge Daly bobbing around like a yo-yo? He enters the room, backs out, sticks his head in, looks us over and disappears again. He isn't even aware I was late.

Finally the bailiff comes to our rescue. "Judge Daly has an emergency case he's trying to settle. He'll be here directly."

We automatically rise when Judge Daly pompously ascends to his glorified seat, without a comment as to his tardiness, and calls the court to order. "Will this be the last witness for the defense?"

Mr. Dowd assures him it is.

"Will the witness please come forward." Awaiting the witness, Judge Daly appears restless.

A tall, willowy young woman glides to the chair Mr. Dowd indicates and after being sworn in by the bailiff, the defense attorney requests she tell the court a bit about herself. She and Karin attended several concerts together before Karin joined the Zen Foundation.

Her name is Roberta Gotto. She met Karin at Tall's Camera shop on Capitol Hill when she'd gone to purchase batteries for her Walkman. They liked the same kind of jazz, mainly Dizzy Gillespie and Arturo Sandoval.

Shoulder length blond hair softens Roberta's features making her look even younger than her twenty-one years. She sits prim and proper with her hands folded in her lap as she describes her relationship with Karin. "We spent time together ... that is before Karin moved into the Zen church. Then I didn't see much of her anymore because she was becoming a Buddhist nun." Using the back of her hand she delicately swept hair from her face.

"She really got interested in Zen and I thought it sounded pretty ... weird, but if it interested her ...then I guessed it was cool."

Judge Daly's bushy eyebrows lift. "Please speak up for the court, Miss Gotto."

I follow Roberta's gaze as she glances over to her former friend. She doesn't appear upset by the fact Karin's on trial for murder. At one time, I caught Karin's slight smile to the witness, but to me, Roberta isn't interested.

Mr. Dowd inquires, "Did Karin ever say or do anything to suggest she was a violent person?"

Miss Gotto flutters a hand in front of her face. "No, oh no, she was the opposite to me. I don't think she could hurt anybody ... not on purpose, anyway."

Mr. Dowd pauses. A perplexed look crosses his face before he asks, "Can you think of any instances, at all, that might give us an idea of what Karin was like when you were with her?"

"Oh, my goodness, let me see ... Yes, there was a time, it was my birthday and she brought me a guinea pig. Most friends ... women, give each other ... you know, something special—a platter of a favorite group, feminine garments, makeup, but she gave me a guinea pig."

Roberta Gotto nervously stated, "She was like that ... always looking out for creepy crawly things, bugs, worms, spiders." Roberta waves her hands in front of her to demonstrate her distaste. "She'd pick up spiders in her bare hands and move them to a safe place." Roberta feigned a shudder.

"But she could make me laugh." Roberta coquettishly cocked her head to one side.

"In what way?" Mr. Dowd encouraged.

"Once she came to pick me up and had her shoes with the laces hung over her ears; another time, she had her blouse pinned to her skirt with clothespins—you know, the pincher kind. She liked to make me laugh; I think it was part of her philosophy … I mean … I think it was, anyway."

"When you heard about Karin and the Zen church, what did you think?"

I notice she sneaked a quick glance at Karin, who was sitting with her head lowered and her eyes closed as though she were meditating.

"I thought … I guess I thought she was really weird. You see, she wouldn't do something like that; she wasn't … I mean this wasn't the kind of person I knew."

The courtroom is silent until Mr. Dowd announces, "I've no further questions, Your Honor."

Judge Daly asks Mr. Clemens if he wishes to cross-examine.

"Thank ya, Yer Honor." Mr. Clemens slowly rises from his chair and pushes it in place before he approaches the witness. "Miss Gotto, Ah'm curious, did ya ever see Karin use drugs?"

We watched Roberta Gotto's face turn pale then infuse to a bright red.

"Miss Gotto," Mr. Clemens gently assures her, "the court isn't interested in whether *ya'll* have used drugs. What Ah'm askin' is … did Karin ever use drugs?"

Roberta glances at Mr. Dowd, who nods it's all right for her to speak. It took her a few minutes to overcome the tremor in her voice. "Yes, sir, sometimes she did."

"Now, Roberta, Ah need ya ta be more specific; how many times did she use them? How often … sometimes … all the time? Can ya hep me with my question?"

Roberta took her time to answer. "Yes, Karin used drugs … I guess you could say she used them pretty heavily. In fact, when the two of us were together, we were high most of the time."

Mr. Clemens presses her further. "What type of serious drugs would ya say the two of ya used most frequently? LSD, mescaline, or just marijuana? Any aphrodisiac Ah'm not familiar with?"

Roberta giggles. "Some of them, mostly marijuana."

Having observed and listened to her, I'm surprised—Karin doesn't appear as a heavy user. In fact, I would not have been able to identify either one of them as having used drugs.

Mr. Clemens, satisfied with Roberta's answers, in his most charming manner thanked her and concluded with, "No further questions, Yer Honor."

A uniformed policeman entered the room through the judge's door, approached the bench and whispered to Judge Daly, who immediately called for a fifteen-minute break.

We remain in our seats while he, the bailiff, and policeman exit the room.

"Wonder what that's all about?" Mike mutters for the benefit of the jurors. "I don't see the Jap family here yet today, has anybody?"

Mary Alice quickly inquires, "Who won the game Saturday night, Mike? You and your kids have a good time?"

"Aw, it was a crappy game; we lost by two. This trial is about as confusing as—"

"Mike, shhh ... zip the lip. Okay?" I suggest.

"I don't know nothin' 'bout drugs, and I sure don't condone 'em. I got kids; I don't want 'em messin' with that junk."

"Mike, someone will hear you and we'll get thrown out of here," another juror lectured him.

"Who's afraid of being thrown out of here?" came Mike's defense.

"Mike, I am, so will you please shut up," I grumble.

"Aw, fer chrissake! I can think of more important things in life than this trial." Mike grabbed hold of both chair arms. I think he planned to leave the room, but Judge Daly returned followed by Ernie, our bailiff.

Back from his business, Judge Daly dismisses the jury for a morning break before a State witness is called.

"I don't for the life of me understand," Laura Judson stammers, "how any legal system can tell its people to keep their mouth shut? I mean this is ludicrous to expect us to go through this every day for hours and not have some verbal exchange with the lawyers, the judge himself, or even among ourselves."

I listen to Mary Alice's agreement that there are things she doesn't understand and getting an explanation would help her better interpret certain issues.

"I guess," I offer, "it all gets said and done behind closed doors when we make the final decision." I excuse myself and walk to the water fountain.

Back in the courtroom, Judge Daly orders the State witness be called.

Mr. Clemens, with a bold smile, invites Dr. Anthony Basta to take the stand.

Dr. Basta is a medium height, middle-aged man, has a bushy mustache, dark hair flecked with gray and piercing black eyes. As Judge Daly resembles a Roman Emperor, this man belongs to the hawk family with his sharp features.

Mr. Clemens begins by asking, "Dr. Basta, if ya would, please tell the court a bit concernin' yer background."

Dr. Basta informs us he's a clinical psychiatrist, who has worked at the Western State Mental Hospital for the past eighteen years.

To me, he looks to be a no-nonsense sort of man I'd want to have around if a psychotic patient got the crazies.

Mr. Clemens interrupts to inquire, "Dr. Basta, in yer eighteen years at a state facility did ya ever treat anyone who was criminally insane? Whose illness … mental illness that is … led them ta be violent, with criminal behavior?"

"Yes, quite a few."

"And Dr. Basta, would ya say any of 'em were schizophrenic?"

We watch the doctor nod. "Generally speaking, schizophrenics do not tend to be violent, but occasionally … there is no set rule. Yes," the doctor pauses as if searching for words. "Yes, I've witnessed schizophrenics turn violent … after a bad spell."

"Dr. Basta, tell the court in yer own words now, if ya will, sir … did ya ever examine and test Karin Colby for schizophrenia?"

Dr. Basta admits he was allowed to examine the defendant, but only once and that he'd been given all the results of the tests administered by the defense's psychiatrist along with all the evidence of the case.

Mr. Clemens suddenly turns back to his cluttered table and searches through an unorganized pile of papers.

His actions and delay create tension in the room; it felt as if a climactic fight was about to ensue. Mr. Clemens finally holds up and rattles a batch of papers. "This is a copy of the report filed by the psychiatrist for the defense. Dr. Jarbouski, … he came ta the conclusion that Karin Colby suffers from chronic undifferentiated schizophrenia.

Now, what Ah'm askin' ya, sir … in yer opinion, Doctor … would ya say this diagnosis is correct?"

"Yep," the witness nods. His right elbow propped on the chair arm, he slowly rubs a hand across his forehead as if wiping away a pain. "She's a schizophrenic, that's for sure."

A sudden commotion draws our attention to the back of the courtroom gallery. The prosecutor's expert witness seems to be corroborating the defense psychiatrist's testimony.

Each morning, from the beginning of the trial, the courtroom is filled to capacity with curious spectators, family members, dozens of journalists and Zen members. The noise intrusion from the gallery forces an angry Judge Daly to pound his gavel in a demand for silence.

The jury quietly waits for the last of the murmurs and whispers to die down. I find the other jurors and myself looking from one attorney to the other for reactions. But both men remain impassive.

Judge Daly's ire crests, he threatens to eject the spectators if there are anymore outbursts in his courtroom. A heavy tension stills the air. Every eye and ear tuned to the weary appearing psychiatrist who has provided us with the most drama in the trial so far.

"Miss Colby is schizophrenic," the doctor repeats as he pushes himself upright in his chair and enunciates his words declaring, "But she isn't insane."

Mr. Clemens was forced to speak above audible whispers heard from the gallery. "Dr. Basta, sir, might ya … could ya explain the distinction for us?"

"Schizophrenia doesn't automatically mean you're insane, anymore than having any other disease means you're dead. The disorder affects people in different ways and in varying degrees. Schizophrenia is not a rare disease.

"Mental illness doesn't come in neat tidy packages, so it's far more common for patients to suffer from a combination of disorders, which makes treating them so complicated."

"Dr. Basta, tell us … Karin is not only schizophrenic … in addition, she shows signs of several personality disorders, the kind seen in violent, antisocial criminals, isn't that so?"

"What you want from me, I assume, is to know whether or not Miss Colby knew what she was doing that day. Did she know she was killing a man, or could she have done otherwise?"

The courtroom suddenly stills, even Judge Daly seems poised for Dr. Basta's summation.

"Yes," came the answer, "Karin did know what she was doing. She suffers borderline symptoms, which means that when she approaches psychosis, she doesn't cross the boundary. Karin Colby is sick all right, but she's far from crazy."

Mr. Clemens looks at us when he asks the doctor, "How can ya be certain that the defendant wasn't psychotic at the time, Dr. Basta? Just what is the evidence, if ya will, sir ... that leads ya ta this conclusion?"

The doctor smiles. "You don't just take the answers on the tests. You look at the whole picture. Let's examine sanity for a moment. Let's take most people ... we feel a gut reaction when we hear of a horrific crime; someone has to be out of their mind, we say. Now, if you commit a horrible, senseless murder ... set a fire or try to kill the President, you would be thought of as crazy. And we still hold people responsible for what they do, don't we?

"Let's be honest here." Dr. Basta shifts forward in his seat. "It's an arbitrary judgment we make. No one really knows if the woman who chops up her husband and cooks him could have done otherwise. Given her genetic structure, her childhood experiences, we really don't know ... do we ... if she could have done better with her life?

"It's the same with Miss Colby. Could she have done better with her life? We don't know. It's impossible to really know, but we must draw the line somewhere, so we say, 'If someone is able to make a rational decision most of the time, then they should be held responsible for their actions.' It's really just common sense, don't you see?"

Dr. Basta becomes animated with his litany. "It's the same for people with mental illness. None of them know the difference between right and wrong, and the exceptions are usually easy to identify.

"A classic example is a woman who every time she sees a certain kind of man in an overcoat suddenly believes he is after her, stalking her. As a result, if a salesman in an overcoat knocked on her front door to sell his wares, she'd shoot him in self-defense. She'd murder him.

"When you get borderline cases, you have to ask ... is the woman really psychotic or is she only indulging her selfish fantasies? In such a situation as the woman I described, or take Karin, you have to look beyond just the regular tests. Dig around and ask yourself, 'What does he or she say about themselves and what of the crime?'

"Do the statements compare with the actual evidence from the crime? Take into consideration the interview, the case history, every little detail ... then you sit back and look at all you've collected. You'd be surprised how often pieces to the puzzle fall into place or how clear a picture forms.

"In this case, a picture emerges of a lonely, insecure, selfish young woman who desperately wanted attention. She showed symptoms of mental illness before the crime, including schizophrenia ... but it's interesting to note, she has a good deal of self-control and awareness. It took a lot of self-control to brandish that heavy piece of wood. It isn't easy for a woman to kill a man with a club. You have to hit at the right time to the right place.

"Karin's a bright woman and thinks pretty clearly. The Zen church encouraged her to *do her own thing*. It's their philosophy from what I've heard. She's not the only one to exercise her way. Remember the Beat poets, how crude they were at poetry reading and how people encouraged them along? It wasn't appreciated and after awhile faded from society. In this case, it's the *Zen way*."

I hear several people snicker at Dr. Basta's reference to the poetry reading, particularly Mike, who snorts out loud. I look over in time to see Mary Alice roll her eyes during his description.

Dr. Basta continues. "Miss Colby's ideas are just too consistent and well thought out to be coming from a psychotic mind. She may well think she's a real psychotic and a genius, but in reality, she showed poor sense.

"The transcripts of Miss Colby's interviews from the police, the psychiatrist, and myself ... if you published everything ... well, I'll bet you'd get people everywhere wanting this woman for their guru, if this is possible. She possesses a clever, dangerous mind."

Doctor Basta's testimony is disturbing, but I don't have much time to consider how it affects my opinion of the case against Karin. *I have so much of my own life to sort out concerning Mark, his mental problems, his health issues and my own family.*

Suddenly it dawns on me, *What if the other jurors notice that the three of us, Laura, Mary Alice and I, are spending lunch and break time together?*

I wait patiently after Judge Daly announces lunch break and leaves his dais. Ernie our bailiff opens the gate and I step aside to let others file out first. By dropping behind I'm able to see if there are any whispers or sidelong glances in Mary Alice's and Laura's direction before I join them.

Mary Alice turns and waits for me to catch up. "Why are you way back there?"

"I was checking to see if any of the others notice how we three spend time together."

Laura pauses. "Oh … yeah. Aw, who cares what they think … do you?"

I wanted to answer yes, to say I can't take a chance of finger-pointing or encouraging any negative suggestions. I don't dare. The trial isn't over … my prayer is that nothing serious happens between now and the end.

I didn't hear Mary Alice's suggestion concerning lunch, but I stumble along with the others. "It's just down here," I hear her explain as we wait for a red light to change.

Chapter 13

On the bus ride home, I've little memory of Mr. Dowd's afternoon cross-examination of Dr. Basta. I heard him attack the doctor's opinion that only a sane person could accomplish a complex psychological view by using Zen to justify an insane behavior.

I do remember Mr. Dowd's exasperation in stating, "Zen is a religion that vigorously encourages people to act impulsively. You are the one, Doctor, who suggested that someone like my client—who you readily agree suffers from a grave mental disorder, who you yourself said stands poised on the fine line between sickness and insanity—can easily cross the fine line under extreme conditions.

"So, what do you think was happening on that religious retreat, where they weren't eating or sleeping and were obsessed with those puzzles?"

Dr. Basta didn't appear upset by Mr. Dowd's attack. I remember watching the doctor rub his cheek and chin before he insisted, "Regardless of what one thinks about Buddhism, Karin Colby knew what she was doing when she killed her Zen Master.

"The proof, for me was," Dr. Basta defended, "according to Karin's enlightenment everything is an illusion. I believe she said she didn't feel any hesitation about what she did and still doesn't feel remorse over killing the man, simply because, in her way of looking at it, she wasn't killing a real man. It was part of a great illusion, of what she calls life.

"The giveaway," Dr. Basta explained, "is that psychotics don't roleplay … it's real to them. Miss Colby claimed all along that what she did was inspired, a religious gesture. I don't buy that for a minute."

My reverie of courtroom proceedings vanish as I feel the bus brake to turn into Park and Ride. In my car heading home, I decide to visit the library this evening. I need to know more about Mark's exposure to Agent Orange. *Is it possible it could cause brain damage resulting in insanity or psychotic symptoms similar to Karin's?*

During dinner I ask, "Anyone game for a trip to the library?" There is little enthusiasm shown, so I decide to go alone as tired as I am—I need facts.

Agent Orange is a new subject for the public. Otherwise, it's known to farmers as DDT and TCDD, an approved herbicide; an extreme toxic dioxin to help rid their food producing fields of insects and weeds.

My search uncovered only two books with any information. *Ranch Hand Trail Dust* explains the military operation between 1962 and 1970. The program goal of the U.S. Department of Defense was to defoliate forested and rural land to deprive guerrillas of cover in Vietnam, Eastern Laos and parts of Cambodia.

A second goal was to induce forced draft urbanization, destroying the ability of peasants to support themselves in the country and force them to flee into U.S. dominated cities, thus depriving the guerrillas of their support bases and food supplies.

Ranch Hand Operation, conducted by the United States Military Forces, sprayed eleven million gallons of an herbicide coded with orange markings on the fifty-five gallon barrels in which it was shipped and became known as Agent Orange.

Air Force records show that by 1970, at least 12 percent of the total area of South Vietnam, had concentration levels, land and water, a hundred times greater than levels considered "safe" by the U.S. Environmental Protection Agency.

Records from the 15th Field Artillery Regiment showed that their men were subject to the fallout of *Rainbow herbicides,* so-called because of the numerous other herbicides used with Agent Orange.

The herbicides were necessary around the perimeters of the bases to keep the concertina (coiled barbed wire) clear of vegetation, provide an open view for sentries on guard duty and along riverbanks to reduce the number of U.S. casualties in the Brown Water Navy.

The maps and graphs in the book had little meaning for me. The second book was a study that linked various diseases to herbicides. The first records stemmed from a study six months after the initial 1962 Ranch Hand Spraying.

When the library lights flash, I realize I've stayed longer than intended. I checkout the book to take home.

After getting the kids off to bed, I wasn't sure I could keep my eyes open to read. The chapter on *Adverse Health Effects* caught my attention but I wasn't able to make it past the first paragraph which read, 'We simply do not know the degree of risk for Vietnam Veterans, that is if there is any.'

When I awake, the clock shows I've only slept a couple of hours. Deep down I worry. Between my duty as a juror, nature of the trial, and my brother-in-law Mark's condition with problems that could possibly be similar, I carry a burden of guilt concerning both issues.

The kids have been so understanding and good, but they will be out of school in a couple of weeks and what then? They think they are too old for a sitter, but I'd need someone responsible with them.

My mind is filled with thoughts. *The foster boys deserve visits with their families; it takes planning to get them together with their siblings, parents or parent. Our plan for a trip to Yellowstone. And what of Glen, who signed up for his vacation the first of June; will he be able to extend his dates or is someone else waiting for him to replace them?*

I toss and turn until I hear the backdoor open and realize it's midnight and I'm wide-awake.

Glen turns with a look of surprise when I walk into the kitchen. "Can't sleep," I mumble, squinting in the bright kitchen light.

He uses one stockinged toe as leverage to kick off his other shoe. At the same time he opens his lunch pail without comment.

"Aren't you glad to see me?" I venture.

He chuckles on his way to the kitchen sink to rinse out his thermos. "At this hour of the morning, you're a fright for sore eyes all right."

I'm thankful we can still banter. I haven't seen much of my husband lately and paid even less attention to his needs. "Busy day?" I inquire. "Want your dinner now?"

"You're gonna be a mess tomorrow without sleep. I would think it important for jury members to stay awake, especially during a murder trial." He ran water into his thermos, sloshed it around, emptied it out and set it on the counter to dry.

"Right, Glen, but I can't sleep. What's going to become of us? The kids are out of school soon, I need to look into visitation for the foster sons, and what about our trip? Will you be able to shuffle your vacation time around? I miss you."

Tears well up and a lump clogs my throat. *Karin Colby has not only committed murder... she's ruining my life and she's unaware of either. Damn her.*

Glen heaves a weary sigh, sits down at the table and removes the foil from his dinner plate. He takes the fork I hand him. "Who told you life was easy?"

"Don't you dare use that *man with one foot* on me."

"No, but Jo, think a moment ... Mark, your sis, this woman you're judging, our kids, and yes, you and me, Jo, we're all problems, but we'll be okay, we just have to be patient and work our way through this. Ummm, pretty good meat loaf; scalloped potatoes, huh? You leave some pretty tasty midnight suppers, woman—only reason I keep you."

Glen is right. I'm unsure which step to take next, which direction to go and what to do first. It's messin' me up.

Glen takes a sip of milk to clear his mouth. "You're not on a Grand Jury so the case must have some time limit."

"I don't know, I don't think anything was ever said about a time limit."

"Well, there's still two weeks before school is out. I'm not worried about the kids, they're almost through; their grades won't change that much."

"Neither boy has overnight visitation privileges," I remind Glen. "If they can get together with their folks and you take them, I'm home in time to pick them up. What happened to the parents fetching and returning their own kids? We're too good to them, Glen."

"When you don't have a car, Jo, six kids strung out from here to there, no money, half the time no spouse, doesn't hurt us to help 'em out. It's the ones that call at two a.m. and get me out of bed to tell me they missed the last bus. Yeah, now that kinda riles me.

"So," Glen toys with his empty glass, "with two weeks ahead, we carry on as we're doing. Okay?" He reaches to caress my cheek. "Might be my turn next to give jury duty and you'll get to run the homestead."

"But, Glen, I don't have to work and support a family, you're doing three jobs. You work, you take care of the kids … un then there's me."

He chuckles. "I'm so busy I forgot about you." He chuckles again. "Better keep Mama happy, 'cause if Mama ain't happy, nobody's happy, right?" He picks up his dishes and heads for the sink.

"I'm going back to bed and sulk," I inform him. "I picked up a book from the library tonight on Agent Orange, think I'll read awhile. Comin'?"

He half turns from the sink. "Maybe a little exercise will help you sleep? I know I always sleep better after a good workout."

"Meet you in bed." I giggle on my way down the hall.

CHAPTER 14

Wednesday morning, the ninth day of jury duty. On the express bus headed into Seattle, I'm surprised how well I've adapted to this daily routine. *If only, when the kids get out of school, the trial is over.*

It's one of our gorgeous May days. Tree branches no longer expose bare limbs; my world is saturated with color and fragrance from exploding blossoms. I enjoy days like this even though I'm stuck indoors, and I have my homework tonight, reading and understanding how Agent Orange is responsible for my brother-in-law's medical and mental condition.

Court is called to order when Judge Daly directs our last witness for the prosecution to come forward. This gentleman is undoubtedly a professional. He solicits respect from head to toe with his neatly trimmed gray hair, tailored suit to fit his slight stature perfectly and expensive black Florsheim wing-tip shoes.

I've never been able to tell the Japanese or Chinese from any other nationality classified as Oriental.

A disheveled Mr. Clemens slowly approaches the witness, Mr. Tohio Toshi, to request that he tell the court something of himself.

"I'm an architectural consultant," Mr. Toshi states, "and I'm director of the New York Japanese Buddha Association. Among other accomplishments, I have several published books and articles regarding the translation of Zen into English."

How strange, I think, *I've never seen Mr. Clemens wear a jacket. It's always draped over the back of his chair and his tie needs straightened.*

"Mr. Toshi, tell us ... did ya know Mr. Nishimura, the murdered founder of the Los Angeles Zen Foundation?"

Mr. Toshi did know the victim. "I met Mr. Nishimura fifteen years ago, just after he came to this country."

"Mr. Toshi, if ya will, sir ... please tell the court, in yer opinion ... was the man qualified ta teach the Buddha Zen?"

"Yes," the witness nods and in a pleasant clear voice states, "Mr. Nishimura was qualified."

"Mr. Toshi ... now ... the defense argues that Mr. Nishimura, by assignin' the puzzle about killin' the Buddha—Ah take it yer familiar with the exercise—provoked Karin Colby ta violence.

"Now, sir, if ya will, please clarify for me un the jury," Mr. Clemens extends his hand to include us, "we're not clear here; ... supposedly, Zen approves of and even encourages impulsive, irrational behavior. So ... please explain ta us ... why Miss Colby should not be held responsible ... that is if Zen drove her ta commit murder. Would ya, sir, comment on that argument for us?"

I'm desperately trying to understand Mr. Clemens' legal reasoning, but he and I don't think alike. Why all this witness explanation over Karin's actions? Either Karin is guilty of murder or she's not. She's sane or she's not. Anyone killing another person, other than in warfare, has to be insane. If in anger, I slap someone, the action is insane and I'm responsible for my insane action. I don't pass the buck or blame to someone else; I'm responsible.

Why is everybody searching for an excuse? Karin bludgeoned her Zen Master and killed him. We do not condone taking the life of another person in the State of Washington. She was insane at the moment, but she killed a man. She committed murder.

Inadvertently, the United States Military killed and maimed their own soldiers. Now they're looking to excuse their action of spreading millions of gallons of a toxic substance coded Agent Orange, contaminating their own men. How can they not be held accountable, responsible? The substance was lethal. Men exposed to the agent are coming home sick and dying. The United States Military committed an insane act, they are responsible.

Mr. Toshi places a hand politely over his mouth to clear his throat. He nods his head graciously and states he will do his best to explain. "It is not easy to determine when religious experiences end and illusions begin." Mr. Toshi's impressive manner lends credence to his speech.

Mr. Toshi explains. "First of all, there is a misconception that Zen is a religion. It is not the worshiping of God or a Supreme Being."

In his relaxed manner he continues. "It is a healing technique for those who worry too much. The purpose is simplistic in a sense that all their worries are represented by one question ... *Why am I not free?*"

He pauses to swallow and gently massages his throat with one hand.

"Mr. Toshi," Mr. Clemens quickly suggests, "the water on yer stand is fresh; perhaps a drink might hep yer dry throat there, sir."

Mr. Toshi quietly drinks from the glass Mr. Clemens indicates. "Thank you, sir." He nods his head towards Mr. Clemens. "I'm fine to continue now."

Mr. Toshi tells a parable. "A carp in a pond is happy swimming around in its domain and doesn't have any worries beyond eating. One day, another carp tells his friend, 'You know what? This pond is only so big, and you are trapped in it. You don't know if you can live outside this pond; you've never been out of it so you can never be free.' Suddenly the fish feels constrained, restricted. The poor carp realizes he *is* trapped ... trapped forever."

Silence cloaks the courtroom during Mr. Toshi's tale. I glance to see Mike, beside me, sitting up and paying attention. Even our Honorable Emperor Daly, elbows on his podium, chin in cupped hand, gives Mr. Toshi his undivided attention.

"Now," Mr. Toshi suggests, "let's talk about human beings. It's a human trait that most people resent the fact they cannot always get their way or do as they like. There are days most of us feel we have no freedoms at all. This is true of the most privileged among us.

"Zen is like a medicine for these days. Zen, the medication, tells you, 'Yes, you are restricted, your mind, your body, your everyday life is limited, constricted by society, but so what? Within these limits are endless variations and opportunities.'

"Zen's purpose is to get you to pay attention and feel involved in your life. You do this with Zen meditation, an exercise for those who want to learn how to make greater strides in the ordinary moments of their lives. Life has limitations and shortcomings; Zen teaches a meditation habit that pays attention to life beyond the extreme moments."

"Thank ya, Mr. Toshi ... but," Mr. Clemens asks, "what about this puzzle? Ta most of us ... Ah take the liberty ta signify most of us ... well sir, it's difficult ta imagine how that puzzle would make anyone more involved in ordinary life. Do ya understand ma statement, Mr. Toshi?"

The witness moves in his chair as if his physical action requires good posture. "First of all, are we not all familiar with the Biblical Story of Jesus when he said if your eye offends you, you should pluck it out? If Christians see something offensive, do they literally gouge out their eyes? No. My opinion is the phrase simply means if you feel an impulse or desire that you know is evil, you make an effort to put the wrong desire out of your mind.

"The koan describing the killing of the Buddha is no different than that. If you are silly enough to daydream about how nice it would be to be an enlightened Buddha and have everyone look up to you as a Master, then that kind of thinking prevents you from fully appreciating yourself for what you are. You'd be like that poor carp wondering what it would be like to swim in a bigger pond and in the process you wouldn't see the opportunities right in front of you.

"Now ... if you say to yourself, 'I'm an ordinary man, I'm nothing like a Buddha, I'll never know what a Buddha experiences.' The koan tells you to banish these thoughts right now; kill this imaginary Buddha, turn your attention back to what is right, to reality, to the present moment, to constructive actions. Who are you right now, you should ask yourself. What are you doing? Think about that. This to me is the meaning of 'If you meet a Buddha in the road, kill him.'"

Mr. Clemens nods his approval. "Thank ya, sir." Then to the judge, "No more questions, Yer Honor." The prosecutor ambles toward his table.

Judge Daly inquires, "Mr. Dowd, do you wish to cross-examine?"

Mr. Dowd rises and slowly approaches the stand. He appears unmistakably watchful, cautious of this witness. "Mr. Toshi," he begins, "do you agree it's possible that a person suffering from a severe mental illness could take the advice of Zen, to accept themselves as they are? Or, would they interpret this to mean, for them, that they should listen to strange voices talking to them … in their head?"

Mr. Toshi nods and responds, "Of course. In fact, I can even think of an example of this happening."

I note Mr. Dowd's hopeful expression, the first since Mr. Toshi took the stand, but a glance in Mr. Clemens' direction reveals his displeasure in the testimony … he's leaning forward, chin in hand, rapidly tapping his pen on the tabletop. It appears he is trying to make eye contact with the witness. However, Mr. Toshi is giving his undivided attention to Mr. Dowd, whose turn it is to question the witness.

"Please proceed, Mr. Toshi."

"Yes, I was a young monk living in Japan when this happened. A student who suffered a nervous breakdown decided to destroy himself and the Zen temple. He set fire to the temple but at the last minute changed his mind about committing suicide. He survived. At his trial, he used the defense that he was motivated by a koan concerning a monk who burned a wooden statue of a Buddha to keep warm one cold night."

Mr. Dowd, now energized, interrupts. "Let me ask you then, Mr. Toshi, you admit that the young man in Japan—due to mental illness, you say—committed a crime after being inspired by a Zen example?

"Then, Mr. Toshi," Mr. Dowd voiced with enthusiasm, "why do you not feel this could have been the same? Why isn't it possible to believe Miss Colby must have been sane?"

"I don't believe I indicated that; I don't believe I said that." Mr. Toshi suddenly appears puzzled at Mr. Dowd's evaluation.

I glance over in time to see Mr. Clemens wince.

"Well," Mr. Dowd replied, "I assume the prosecutor put you on the stand to support his position that Miss Colby was sane when she committed the crime. Or am I, sir, mistaken about this?"

Mr. Toshi's conduct is gracious and under control. "I'm not sure, Mr. Dowd, what you wish of me. It is my understanding I am to answer questions about Zen Buddha practice. I'm not qualified to judge Miss Colby's state of mind or condition."

Mr. Dowd is at once uncomfortable, his enthusiasm gone; he nods. "I see, then you acknowledge that Miss Colby could have been pushed into her psychotic episode by the activities during the Zen retreat?"

"But, of course. Personally, I hope this is the case. There is always hope her illness can be treated. I would like to predict that Miss Colby could someday be a benefit to society rather than a burden."

"Mr. Toshi," Mr. Dowd faces the jury, "I cannot agree more." Turning back to Mr. Toshi, "Thank you, sir." He then turns to Judge Daly. "No more questions, Your Honor."

Judge Daly calls for a morning recess.

I leave the jury gallery depressed, relating what Mr. Toshi said to Mark's case. Since he returned from Vietnam, Mark's life isn't like a fish in a pond and there is no comparison to Karin's case … however, they both deal with mental dysfunction.

I wonder if Mark could be convinced to become a Buddha … but he can't, he married, and besides, he's not bald enough.

"Jo," Mary Alice breaks into my thoughts, "I think I need to get drunk. Laura laughed at the idea. But this case is getting interesting, I'll say that much for it."

Mike saunters up to the three of us. "Discussin' the case, are you?"

"No, Mike," Mary Alice says, "just wishin' for a better life. All that sunshine out there and look at us in this fishbowl."

Mike asks, "You believe in fate?"

I'm prompted to inquire, "Why do you ask?"

Mike replies, "You know what? It seems like fate is happening in there." He indicates the courtroom. "I was worryin', thinkin' maybe I wasn't qualified to do this. But someone has to decide what's right and wrong."

"If anyone overhears you," Mary Alice mumbles, "we've just been declared a hung jury … is that the right term? Or else we're gonna be thrown out for discussing the case in public."

I head for the courtroom. "We better get back and see if we're still jurors."

The morning moves along at an unbearably slow pace. Testimonies and evidence at last finished, there is only the closing arguments to listen through before starting our deliberation.

Mr. Dowd begins first by reminding us Karin Colby suffers from a mental disease. "This is an irrefutable fact," he stresses. "The only real question is if we should send this mentally ill young woman to a hospital or to prison?"

My mind refuses to stay at attention. If I'm asked my opinion, I'm apt to say, 'Who gives a damn? To me, this is a lost cause. Look at the money we taxpayers waste, the time spent on one particular person when there are others who become lost causes, who are expected to drop out of sight without disturbing anyone.' I'm so disgusted with this legal procedure. Karin has never said a word in her behalf. She committed murder.

The only part of Mr. Dowd's speech, I confess, that caught my attention was the ending.

"I have a reason for believing," Mr. Dowd said, "that Karin didn't know what she was doing that day." He pauses to make eye contact with each of us before he states, "Do you remember during the voir dire when Mr. Clemens dismissed anyone who had a relative with mental illness or was connected to mental health? There was a reason for this.

"If anyone in your family has such a problem. You know how awful it is. How innocent these people with the affliction are and how everyone suffers, particularly the one affected."

Mr. Dowd, in a lowered voice, admits, "I am not qualified to sit in that jury box with you. Do you realize that Mr. Clemens would have kicked me out? I happen to have a brother, who came home from Vietnam this year, diagnosed with a mental condition. It's destroying his life, and it isn't his fault. He left to serve our country in perfect health, or he would never have been accepted in the military. I'm watching his life fall apart. I know what it does to a person and I know what it does to me inside." He taps his chest to emphasize his point.

"Karin Colby's future and the fate of other innocent people are in your hands." Mr. Dowd pauses, rubs his forehead with one hand then drops his arm back to his side. "All I ask is that when you come to your final decision … judge her, but ask yourself this one question, "What verdict in this case best protects and enhances our lives? Justice is meant to protect and enhance the lives of good people in our society.

"Will keeping a dangerously ill woman locked away in a cell for an arbitrary period of time keep a woman away from society? Will putting her in a secure hospital for as long as it takes to heal her serve society? This becomes a difficult question to answer doesn't it?

"Remember, Karin Colby has been judged insane by a qualified specialist. I have defended her on this basis, by evaluations and other evidence. Karin has not resisted her defense. She refused the services of a private lawyer. She told me she did not want her mother to have to pay for a counselor. Karin, herself, alleges, 'I don't need to be defended because there's nobody here to defend.'

"Karin is not someone who committed a crime and thought she could get away with it. She admits she is insane. The day I met Karin, I could tell immediately that something was terribly wrong; the first thing I did was hire a psychiatrist to evaluate her. On the basis of the evaluation, I chose the insanity defense.

"If you feel any resentment from having to sit through this insanity defense trial, blame me for it; do not blame Karin. She honestly thinks the outcome if this trial is utterly irrelevant.

"She is now, as she was on that fateful day, clearly insane and is unable to grasp the significance of what she has done. She does not recognize the difference between right and wrong. To put her in jail would be like throwing a five-year-old in jail. It will not bring Mr. Nishimura back to life, it would not be a punishment, it would be meaningless. I honestly believe this."

Once again, my opinion changes. Mr. Dowd, though I find him a weak defense attorney, does show compassion and understanding of a problem I'm facing ... we in society face.

Have we always had men and women return from war so mentally afflicted as Mark? How is it possible for him to face a fair trial? We, the jury, are not qualified to judge another's mental condition, only their acts. Mark is yet to be tried, but who knows what lurks in his mind. He served time in the military. Is he a casualty of war?

Though I think Mark is innocent, is he really? Has his mental attitude become deranged? Or has it something to do with his Agent Orange exposure?

Judge Daly consults his wristwatch and wall clock before he announces, "We will resume further closing after lunch." He gathers his papers, adjusts his great wings about him and departs the room without a backward glance.

Wonder if he's as drained of energy as I am? I don't even feel animosity toward his Esteemed Honor, even though I harbor resentment of being intimidated by these men who aspire to lofty legal positions.

My experience with people who practice law is that they maintain control over others who are less perfect and get away with cruel innuendoes and remarks. Mark so well described his Mr. Dennis as an example. Mark, out of innocence, didn't take his arrest as anything more than a misjudgment against him, but Mr. Dennis came across like Mark is a subhuman creature. He showed little patience with Mark, a human being, who maintains he did nothing as deplorable as Mr. Dennis suggests.

From early childhood, I was taught women have suffered for generations at the hands of an unfair legal system and we're still recognized as second class citizens.

King Solomon, to me, was the wisest judge that ever ruled. How great was his wisdom when he settled the child issue between the two women?

'Cut the child in half,' he advised, 'and give a half to each mother.' Cruel? Oh no, he was wise. He knew the real mother, for the sake of her baby's life, would be willing to forfeit her child to the other woman.

"Jo!" Mike catches himself before he stumbles over me, "move. The bailiff's not gonna stand there holdin' the gate open all day. What's the matter with you?"

"Sorry." I scramble to my feet and through the open gate. Embarrassed, I don't look back at my fellow jurors who are held up because of my daydreaming.

So much is at stake. Karin's trial is about to end. Mark's still to begin. I've papers to prepare for my congressman, senator and several women's organizations concerning men dying from exposure to the fatal Agent Orange.

My family deserves my attention and care; they are my responsibility. *Please God,* I pray the words I've heard somewhere, *give me the strength to accept what is mine and the wisdom to leave what isn't. Give me the wisdom to change what I can and the wisdom to leave what I can't.*

The three of us head for a quiet corner, the rustle of paper bags the only sound outside of weary sighs. The companionship is comforting, but our thoughts belong to us alone.

"Hey gals," Mary Alice jests before biting into her peanut butter sandwich, "you're having fun now, aren't you?"

I feel more relaxed after a good laugh. This isn't exactly what Zen practice would suggest, but anticipation of the decision ahead of us isn't exactly normal or routine either.

CHAPTER 15

I open my front door to chaos … each child demanding my undivided attention. I sense supper isn't ready. The fellows refuse to set the table, while the girls argue over which to cook first, the hamburger patties or the vegetables.

Once organized, the girls propose supper served outside with the bugs that will invite themselves to the food and us. The boys opt for paper plates and plastic ware.

Thankfully the phone was quiet until after dinner but made up for it later. Dear Great-Aunt Clara called to give a repeat description of her jury duty back in the year 1907. "They kept us sequestered back then." Her shrill voice rehashes the past. "We stayed in Seattle's best hotel, played cards most of the night and ate like kings. They treated us like royalty."

I wanted to remind her that such luxury is what probably bankrupted the judicial system of today, but I politely listen and comment when necessary.

I wonder if she is aware that long before there were juries, our nation was ruled by magistrates who served as judge and jury? Cost effective. Of course a lot of witches were burned at the stake and people tarred and feathered back then too.

Somewhere in time it was decided we should be judged by peers, people equal to ourselves. However, in picking a jury, people are selected by the attorney's discretion. The accused has the right to ask for a specific juror or to have one disqualified, but usually the jury members are selected by the trial lawyers. I certainly don't consider Karin my peer, but Mark, my brother-in-law is family and I'd never be selected to hear his case.

Mr. Dowd surprised us jurors when he stated, "I would not have been chosen if the prosecuting attorney knew my situation."

I too would have been thrown out along with Mr. Dowd if my circumstances were known.

Aunt Clara finishes her summation of jury duty and with her usual cheery platitudes voices her good-bye and hangs up.

Why, I wonder, is it conceivable we citizens are chosen as peers to a criminal?

The jury system may have been intended as an honest means to represent the accused but I find it revolves around who is the most convincing, conniving lawyer with the best command of the English language.

I personally don't feel the prosecution or the defense speak in terms the common person understands. They are taught to evoke sentiment and emotions in their favor.

They translate the defendant's actions without having been a participant. My contention is, we are not educated to fully understand the justice system, and the court does not have time to give us a bona fide course in law. It takes years to study and understand the judicial system. Most jurors are no more qualified to judge than they would be to take over a surgeon's position.

I'm not educated to know what to retain and what is unimportant. My education has not dealt with abnormal human behavior. Any misjudgment I make must remain with me the rest of my life. Lawyers are blameless where a jury verdict is involved.

After the final verdict, their alibi will be, 'It was in the hands of the jury.'

The judicial system is well versed in the tricks of their trade, while my world revolves around being a good citizen. I do not have the appropriate terminology to address military, clergy, or the court.

It's God's place to run this world, not mine. And this isn't a cop-out on my part. It's admitting ... there but for the grace of God go I.

I'm sitting here with papers spread out on the kitchen table that testify to hours of research the government doesn't dispute concerning Agent Orange exposure to American soldiers but neither does it offer a solution to rectify the damage, which to me is a form of denial. Why so little research before the toxic agent was used?

Men cared for in U.S. Military institutions across America, with diagnosed valid symptoms, must suffer in silence until such a time as there is money and time to work out a program for their benefit. The war is over; no one is concerned with the past but the victors.

Our judicial system does little to help the victims. Men in power are busy with more popular government projects. Besides, an underpaid serviceman offers little to fill politicians' coffers or bring them fame.

Until demands are made of the government to represent the afflicted by either the military or the President, men such as Mark may never live long enough to see their families raised or live till their retirement.

It's been a busy day; I dread tomorrow. Life was much easier when I didn't have the weight of one woman's life in my hands and so little knowledge to help Mark. How insignificant, how powerless I am.

Wednesday night's TV does little to capture the kids' interest. They come in after dark to request if friends can sleep outside with them overnight.

My urge is to deny them, but why must they sacrifice on my account? Had I been honest at the beginning of the trial and been excused, I wouldn't be in this position I created for myself.

Why did I take on more than I had a right to handle? Why did I make it my duty to make a judgment against a woman who I'm not sure is guilty or insane? Do I honestly care what becomes of Karin? But then again, am I prepared to subject her to a death sentence? Hanging? Am I strong enough to request this for her?

"Sure, you betcha," I tell the kids, "but you know the rules, fellas." Then I remind them, "No loud noises to bother the neighbors."

Bother the neighbors? Suddenly an idea flashes to mind. *Paula was told not to confront or bother Kathy, the teenage accuser of Mark, but I wasn't. Why not? What have I got to lose?* Then as suddenly as it occurs to me, I realize I can't, *not till the trial is over. I could ruin everything I've worked to hide by blundering in and stirring up a hornets' nest.*

I collect my papers with figures and graphs from accumulated facts by politicians. I've compiled symptoms of strange maladies and ailments of men who have returned from Vietnam. I even have maps of areas that are barren wasteland that will never grow a single blade of grass due to deep contamination. Yet, I have collected so little information.

The wheels of justice will not turn unless someone makes them move. I am one person against a multitude. Poor Mark, he gave so much for his country and must suffer forever because of poor government judgment. And who is guilty?

Before I turn in for the night, I peek outside to observe the boys. Boys settle down better than girls, who will chatter all night, prowl the house, get into my makeup, giggle, make racket, continuously eat and keep the household awake throughout the night.

I pause to take in the star-studded peaceful night and give thanks for my children. Suddenly, for no reason, a case during the summer of 1959 in Jackson, Michigan comes to mind.

A teenage girl and her twelve-year-old brother, angry over being refused a request, ignited their parents' bed while they slept. The mother and father suffered burns over fifty percent of their bodies.

They were children. I never heard the outcome of the trial, or what became of them. I wonder at the attorney who had to represent those children.

The attorneys who represent my foster children are always new to the bar with little court experience and achieve little beyond giving the kids an embossed card with a name and phone number while adding, 'Should you need help or have questions.' To my knowledge, none of my wards have ever called these court representatives, who remain ghost figures to them.

We see little of these counselors outside of court appearances when the parents make a lifestyle change or the court sees fit to unite the family.

Again, there is little money or fame for these court appointed legal representatives who are looking for better paying clients.

I scribble a quick note concerning the backyard full of sleeping boys for Glen when he comes home.

'Please leave the light over the stove on for them when you come to bed.' As an afterthought, I pen, 'Sorry, but too tired for any late night workout. Hope you understand. Love you.' I draw a heart at the bottom of the note and write 'me' inside.

CHAPTER 16

A beautiful warm June morning, the tenth day of Karin Colby's trial. Yesterday we finished hearing closing statements and deliberated on phase one, the *guilt* phase.

This Thursday morning, we assemble in the jury room to decide phase two of Miss Colby's proceedings. We found Karin guilty of murder in the first phase and now must decide her sanity.

Our deliberations begin with a foreman selection as was done previously. Mr. Donaldson declines this time, said he's already taken a turn. He nods to Mr. Washington. "Dwayne, if no one objects, why don't you do it for us?"

Dwayne Washington is a young, black ex-Marine. "If no one else wants to volunteer," he suggests. When no hand is raised, he accepts. "Let's start with the same secret ballot Mr. Donaldson had us do last time."

I write 'undecided' and quickly fold my paper. I'm not ready to make a stand. I glance up to see the others have already voted, folded and passed along their ballots. I can hope others vote as I do.

Mr. Donaldson opens each ballot and reads aloud to Dwayne who tallies them on a yellow legal pad. "Eleven votes for sanity," Dwayne announces. "One undecided."

Mrs. Marshall, a housewife, asks, "Do all twelve of us have to make the same verdict?"

"Yes," Dwayne replies then fingering his lower lip with one hand and tapping his pencil tip on the table with the other, he addresses Mrs. Marshall further, "Yes, ma'am, that's what the judge said. It's a murder trial … has to be unanimous."

A whispered "oh, no" from Mrs. Marshall is loud in the silent room.

I catch myself before I smile. *Wonder if everyone will assume the undecided vote is Mrs. Marshall's?*

"The next step then, I guess," Dwayne sighs, "is to go over the evidence. We'll go around the room and list all the main points, then we'll vote again to see if the vote changes." Sitting back in his chair, he tents his fingers in front of his chest.

"Let's begin on this side." He gestures to Ryan on his right. "You wanna begin, Ryan?"

Ryan, the street maintenance manager, asks, "Why don't we just ask how each voted? Then the one voting 'undecided' can explain their reason."

I sense Ryan doesn't like taking instructions from Dwayne. Ryan is such a jerk, worse than Mike.

Hanna, a short, stout, black hotel maid faces Ryan with a frown. "The jury instructions suggest we do it this way. I say we do it like Dwa… uh… Mr. Washington asks, there's a reason we do it this way."

Mr. Donaldson nods. "It's too early to poll the jury. Let's do it the way Dwayne suggests."

"What is it we're doing now?" Mary Alice grumbles. "I'm sorry but I'm confused."

Dwayne patiently explains as several people inhale and exhale loudly. "Mary Alice, we are going to start reviewing the evidence that suggests Miss Colby is sane then we will talk about the evidence that suggests she's insane."

A nervous Laura Judson pipes up, "I guess I'm the dumb one. None of the rest of you ever ask questions. I'm not going to complain like I did last time. so I'll just shut up."

"You're not dumb," Linda, the daycare aid says. "Honey, you just go right ahead and ask questions till you understand. Okay?" She pretends not to notice the withering glance Dwayne tosses her way.

"Should somebody take notes?" asks Sara, the young, pretty substitute teacher. "I would think it might make things easier."

Dwayne approves the idea. "Anyone want to volunteer? C'mon folks, someone help me out here." Then to Sara, "C'mon, give me a hand."

"No siree, I'm just serving my sentence of jury duty." Sara declines.

"C'mon, Sara," Mike prods. "You can do it, you know how to write fast."

"No, Mike, thank you very much. Pick on someone else, okay?"

Sensing the start of an argument between Mike and Sara, I speak up, "I'll do it." *This will give me a chance to think things out more clearly.*

Dwayne shoves the yellow pad and a pen in my direction. "I'll start first," he offers. "Then we'll go around the table with Ryan next."

Everyone politely listens as he shares his ideas. "Let me say … I favor the second psychiatrist who said, 'Miss Colby is sick … but not crazy.' The psychiatrist thought Karin Colby definitely did know what she was doing."

"Yeah," Harry, the gardener, interrupts. "And what about how expertly she swung that heavy wooden stick? Someone nuts woulda been swinging like crazy, panicking, going wild."

When Harry pauses for a breath, Ryan quickly adds, "I agree with Harry. Karin Colby is normal. She went to school, even passed college exams and spent some time in the Peace Corps, didn't she? She was sane enough to talk her mother into letting her live at home rent free, goof-off, smoke pot. Sounds pretty normal to me until that day."

Hanna is convinced the drugs were responsible. "Even if she wasn't doin' 'em that day. I know people who do drugs and stop, but there's still somethin' wrong with their minds. Like I knew these people before they got messed up and they was decent folks, in control of themselves. Most of 'em are pretty calm people, but once they's been on dope, uh-uh; ever after, theys minds er different."

"You know what just came to mind?" Mike interrupts. "It's if Karin really thinks she's a spiritual god and she doesn't care where she goes or what happens to her, this is all insignificant to her … we might as well vote her into jail. And," Mike punctures the air with his forefinger, "if Karin's just faking that she's crazy, then she's guilty and it won't make a damn bit of difference … so let her pay the price."

"Thanks for the rundown, Mike." Dwayne's frustration is beginning to show. "But we need to answer the question: Is she sane or insane?"

Ryan answers my uncertainty when he states, "We can't prove what's in the gal's head, Dwayne." He looks around for approval. "To me, we can only guess as to what seems best ... let's send the twit to jail."

I've had this suspicion from the beginning as to why Karin is kept from testifying. It would be a confession and a confession could mean she is guilty, regardless of sanity or insanity. We jurors must have faith in the legal system and our convictions must be stronger than the fear of making a wrong decision.

We can't ask questions during the trial concerning facts we don't understand. We are not allowed to take notes to help reinforce our decisions later. How can the others not see court is simply a play acted out between lawyers, and in the final analysis it will be the judge who will make the decision as he interprets the law.

Dwayne's anger erupts. "If we can't decide whether Karin's sane or not, then we have to tell the judge. This is better, by far, than making a decision for the wrong reason."

"I thought we weren't ready for arguments yet," Mrs. Marshall reminds us. "Let's try to stay with the subject or we're never going to get through with this. We need to get back to talking about the evidence."

"Thank you, Mrs. Marshall." Dwayne mops his brow hastily with a retrieved handkerchief. "Can we get on with this now?" He indicates Mary Alice on his left.

"Thanks, Dwayne. What I'm questioning is ... when Karin got tackled to the floor, she didn't complain. She was handcuffed, they busted her, but still she didn't resist. She was dragged off to jail, talked to her lawyer, and supposedly all those doctors. What stumps me is her sitting in the courtroom for how long ... over a week, while people talk in front of her about how crazy she is. I'd be a basket case."

Mary Alice continues. "This is pretty stressful. But Karin? She's calm, cool as a cucumber ... in control. If a person is insane, don't they lose control? Would and could you endure all this? And ... here's another thing. If she is insane, she might very well appear in control to confuse us, when really she doesn't feel on the inside what she demonstrates outwardly to us. Know what I mean? I don't understand her being declared out of control; I think she's got great resilience."

Mary Alice gestures she's finished. Dwayne nods to Mr. Donaldson.

"Here's what baffles me," Mr. Donaldson explains, "Karin admits to killing her teacher as the answer to the puzzle. My gut reaction tells me she knew what she was doing. Therefore where's the argument? I pass."

"Harry," Dwayne asks, "what do you think?"

The gardener scratches his head and massages his chin. "I'm trying to make sense of all this, but I can't think of anything right now; I'll be thinkin' while I'm listenin'."

Dwayne looks at me. "You ready?"

"It bothers me her being able to sit still, in complete controlled silence, every day for nearly a year. That means hours at a time, long before the fatal episode took place. To me, this is something an insa… er… a schizophrenic would never be able to do. But then I'm not an authority on the temperament of a schizophrenic. I pass."

"Linda, you've had little to say." Dwayne gently reminds her.

Linda's charm is her low husky voice. "I don't like the fact she didn't get to testify. She's the one accused, after all. Does this mean her lawyer finds her too dysfunctional to take the stand? I feel the lawyers are trying to hide something. It's difficult for me to judge if she's sane or not. I guess I need more enlightenment."

Several in the room chuckle. A perplexed look moves across Linda's face. Dwayne sensing her confusion, explains, "Linda, if you recall, the word *enlighten* is the word the attorneys used as Karin's excuse for killing her teacher." Linda's face stains with color as she quickly lowers her head into her hands.

Laura Judson is next. It's obvious she's nervous, she fidgets before she states, "I agree with everything everyone's said, but, what I don't understand is how are we supposed to remember all the stuff said in court … by heart?"

Laura's question voices my sentiment. Jurors are not educated to know what facts to keep and what to overlook. We forget which truths versus which alibis. It's confusing when the lawyers strut out their special picked witnesses, then coerce, threaten and exhibit evidence. We've heard nothing to back the innocence from the witnesses whose testimonies we are to consider factual.

The lawyers and witnesses didn't view the act; they are relating their interpretation. To me, this is not fair to the accused, only an assumption, told as the lawyers want it heard.

The attorneys may say their evidence is accountable, obtained from the victims. But in Karin's case, it lacks common sense and remains baffling to me, a juror who desires clarification on many issues. The direct questions posed to the witnesses are aimed, of course, to better the lawyer's viewpoint.

I feel I'm abused by my part in the legal system. Jury duty falls to those of us unable to avoid it. We jurors are manipulated by deceitful, scheming and fraudulent means employed by those with far greater understanding of how to handle Karin's case.

We are made to feel this trial revolves around us. Yet, in reality, our opinions are the last ones considered; we are ignorant of the legal system.

Behind closed doors in the jury room, little explanation comes to us, only the reminder, 'Your instructions were explained to you; follow them.' Is it any wonder the jury has problems coming to the same verdict. Why not just vote guilty and get the trial over.

I need time to think; I'm not prepared to make a final decision. The entire trial moved along so agonizingly slow and now it's moving too fast. We have been here only a short time and already I feel as if everyone wants to be done with it and vote whichever way brings a unanimous decision so we can leave.

"I just thought of something." Harry raises his arm. "Karin's a smart lady ... ya'll said so. It seems to me like she's too normal. She walks and talks like she's normal. I can tell when someone's crazy, they act strange, different ... not normal. They aren't smart like Karin acts."

The room is suddenly silent. I shove the notepad with the pen down the length of the table, towards Dwayne who stops the pad with the palm of his hand. "Okay folks, here's a list in behalf of Karin's sanity. Now, let's talk about the evidence that suggests she's insane." He tears my note sheets from the pad and slides it back to me.

Dwayne begins, "Whether we think Karin acted like a real crazy person or not, the woman is schizophrenic; both doctors agreed. So we're not talking of someone who just up and says 'I suddenly went crazy.' Karin experienced less and less control as the years passed, even though she managed to keep out of trouble. It's our responsibility to make a decision, based on evidence, if she has a mental disorder as diagnosed and if she will be tried as being mentally deficient.

"Remember now," Dwayne reminds us, "this gal with a mental disorder was living at the church under strict disciplinary rules. She lived with little sleep and endured hour after hour of silent sitting. I believe it was the first doctor that impressed me with the idea that living like that, a normal person would go nuts."

"Can't we take a quick break?" an anxious Mrs. Marshall requests.

"No," snaps Mr. Donaldson. "We are permitted time out for bathroom breaks only; otherwise, we stay in this room until we reach a verdict."

Earlier, before we entered the jury room, Judge Daly allowed us to make the necessary calls to notify our families we would be unavailable until we reach a verdict.

Great-Aunt Clara's comment comes to mind. *'We were sequestered, taken out for a meal...'* No mention concerning meals was made during Judge Daly's instructions. Lunch doesn't pose a problem, most of us carry sack lunches.

"No one said we couldn't take a ten minute break," Sara said. "I'm going to have a nicotine fit and several will agree with me if we don't get a cigarette pretty soon."

"We all use the bathroom, it's going to take longer than a ten minute break," Mary Alice reminds us as she heads in that direction.

During time out, others paced aimlessly around the room. I sat transfixed, my eyes closed, head in hands, trying to analyze my thoughts.

What is it the others aren't concerned about that bothers me? I could care less about Karin Colby, but I am not going to be coerced into voting her guilty of anything.

I'm aware of Dwayne's voice at the jury room door. I glance back to see he's conversing with the bailiff. *Could it be Dwayne has changed his mind and is ready to give up?*

"Does someone have the judge's instructions?" I ask.

If I were sure in my mind of Karin's sanity, I'd agree with the others, which I'm tempted to do anyway. I want this trial to end as much as they do, but something makes me feel that Karin is insane. But then, does that mean Mark, lovable, sweet Mark is insane and forced himself on a young girl, an innocent child?

Where does this gut sensation come from that makes me feel Karin is insane? Why is my mind void? Why can't I concentrate?

The more my thoughts wander around aimlessly, the more confused and frustrated I become. Leaning back in my chair, I decide I'm going to put the whole issue to rest. *I need to stop thinking about it; I need to get away from the entire matter—if only it were possible, but obviously it isn't to be.*

Okay, okay. I rub my forehead and temples to ease my stress. *When the others return to the table, I'm going to confess my reason for voting 'undecided'.*

CHAPTER 17

We slowly return to our seats after a brief break to await instructions from Dwayne.

I've been foolish and irresponsible. I admit to being so absorbed in my outside life, it comes as a revelation to realize how little attention I'm paying to my duty as a juror for Karin.

I blame my spaced-out mind for ignoring the importance of coming to terms with Karin's insanity. I approach Dwayne to explain my sudden connection between Karin and my undecided vote.

Dwayne clarifies for the jurors my decision to vote undecided before he nods for me to proceed. I'm gathering weak courage to face those before me, when the bailiff unannounced boldly enters the room.

"Sorry, I need lunch orders." He apologizes for the intrusion. "Fill out these slips and get them back to me as soon as possible. Box lunch choices are chicken, turkey, ham, tuna or a vegetarian. Just X the box and sign the slip, please."

"How much this gonna cost me?" Mike inquires.

"It's on the house," the bailiff informs him. "Have someone knock on the door for my attention when you're finished."

Mary Alice and I exchange a wink and smile. *Yay, free meal*. Our homemade lunches have suddenly lost any appeal.

Dwayne, on his way to deliver the lunch slips to the bailiff, suggests, "If there are no more interruptions … Joella, tell us your concern."

I clear my throat to nervously begin. "The reason I voted undecided is, there have been times I've acted irresponsible. I've done things I would never do under normal circumstances. It surprised even me afterwards, but I was still guilty.

"Karin Colby is classified as sick, her mind deranged by a disease. From the time she grew up, she's been a lonely young woman, drifting about for a couple of years, becoming more and more socially inept. Then she finds this church, it's a haven to this lost, lonely woman. I see a dysfunctional woman struggling to make herself accepted into their confusing, outrageously strict disciplined philosophy.

"She wouldn't have understood what she was getting herself into or what she was doing. She made a decision alone, or thought she had to. I think what we've heard from witnesses and testimonies, my rationale of her is … Karin is a person who has lost her mind. So, I think it best, in my interest, to judge her insane. This removes the undecided from the ballot."

"Can you explain yourself?" Ryan smirks. "I mean … sounds like you identify with her … like how, care to give us some details?" His remark brings a few sniggers from around the room.

"Out with it," Mike mocks. "Don't hold back."

I ignore their remarks and turn the question back on them. "You have never done something wrong or unnecessary? What if you see something so vile … no, that's not what I want to say. It's difficult for me to describe a good example. A situation … take a situation so stressful that you said or did something you regretted but couldn't explain yourself afterwards."

"Ma wife does that all the time." Mike's interjection induces laughter.

I continue, "This is why I reason Karin is capable of her behavior. She's been mentally exhausted for years, even drugs didn't help. Then, at last, she thinks she's found herself. She puts the effort and time into going through a retreat that even we can't understand. You don't think it makes sense that eventually she would lose control of herself? She would break down mentally, have a nervous breakdown?"

I see a few heads nod in understanding. "It makes sense," Geraldine, a parts expediter from the Renton Boeing plant, agrees. "But… my confusion is the judge said 'We are not supposed to decide concerning possibilities. We have to be sure she's insane in order to acquit her.' What you're saying makes me apprehensive with my decision, it becomes a possibility."

I look over at Dwayne who is focusing on the papers I gave him earlier. *Do I dare hope for his support?*

After a brief hesitation, he looks down the length of the table at me, bringing his elbows to rest in front of him. "And … I have come to a conclusion," he says. "From the beginning of this trial, I've felt Colby's mental problems are not a good enough excuse for what she did."

"The prosecutor, Mr. Clemens, made sense. I didn't think Mr. Dowd did … I felt he was playing Karin up for the sake of getting her off the hook. Mr. Dowd just didn't make me feel sure or certain … so I voted her sane; in other words, guilty in the part two phase."

Dwayne, with palms up, gestures a submissive attitude. "I admit, I want her punished. I believe that if a man kills another man for no good reason, then such a man should be punished at the full extent of the law; in this case, it's a woman.

"It makes sense to me. I was even hoping everyone would vote like I did, then my conscience would be clear." He leans back in his chair and strokes his chin before crossing his arms. "Then," he continues, "here comes this one undecided vote and my conscience is no longer eased. Now, I'm going to have to re-examine my thoughts before I convict Karin Colby of murder. What you just said, Joella, makes sense."

Dwayne lapses into a momentary silence, then begins to explain. "During the time I was in the service, I knew a man who *lost it* all of a sudden. We were in Vietnam … a lot of men were *losing it* back then." He draws in a slow deep breath and concentrates on his thumbnail before he makes eye contact again.

"This guy … he was my buddy, a soul brother. One day he was sane … calm as could be, but—" Dwayne pauses again, lifts his face upward as if he's beyond his immediate setting. "Yep, the cat, he lost it." In a soft voice, he continues, "He went completely crazy. He annihilated every last person around him. He shot … killed a lot of innocent people."

Staring straight ahead Dwayne admits, "I know this can happen … I witnessed it." He hurriedly wiped a hand across his eyes, down his cheek to his chin. "I know… I was there … it happened."

We quietly watch Dwayne gain control of his emotions. "The point I have now is … and, Geraldine, you are correct to point it out; we have to be certain. Right now … I can't honestly say I'm certain anymore, but I'm not convinced I should convict her either."

The room is quiet until Geraldine inquires, "Joella, using your example, did I understand you to say Karin couldn't control herself that day? I understand where you're coming from about losing control … I'm guilty of doing impulsive things in my life.

"But," she slowly draws out her words, "isn't the main issue here whether or not Karin knew she had killed? Excuse me … let me put it this way," she stammered, "she had planned to kill that man. You don't think she was aware of what she was doing? From her confessions to the doctors and the police, my reaction is… she knew very well what she'd done."

"Yes," Linda agreed. "We can't say she was in control, we don't have to. The question to us is … was Karin aware she'd killed somebody?"

"Exactly," Harry chirped.

I watch Mr. Donaldson nod his head. "Uh-huh. I'll go along with this."

"Yeah," Mike pipes up, "me too."

I open the copy of the judge's instructions. "Yes, it would seem this way, but listen to this … Judge Daly has underlined the word *legal* insanity. He even states … here, let me read to you. 'A person if legally insane, as a result of mental disease or defect, lacks substantial capacity of either—' Judge Daly also underlined the word *either*, 'to appreciate the criminality of their conduct or to perform their conduct to the requirement of the law.' The word *or* is underlined too."

"So," Dwayne interprets, "the words *either* and *or* give us some slack here; do we agree?"

Ryan vigorously shakes his head. "Hey, gang, maybe Karin is able to substantiate herself to the law for every other moment of her life, and yes, including killing the Buddha. But … I ask you, why should we believe that just for one instant she's insane? Just for that one second act … why, this might give her press, honor her as important, give her prestige as an outstanding guru over all gurus. You don't see her perfectly timed act as her moment of instant insanity?"

"Yeah," Mike agrees. "But how do we prove it?"

"Never thought of it that way," someone says.

"You know," Harry states, "it's like if a person has been doing a stupid job all his life and he gets jealous of his boss or some guy higher up than him. So he up and says, 'Hey man, I went crazy, but I'm okay now; I didn't mean any harm, I'm okay now. So how 'bout I take over this dude's job I just done in. You don't mind now, do you?'"

"Yeah," Ryan growls, "how about this: Karin gets released from the hospital or insane asylum, whatever, in a couple of years. Then she's free to start her own cult, or what the hell you call them people … the ones who like her and think her way is cool."

"I agree," Mike excitedly exclaims. "I know people like this. One minute they're okay and the next thing you know, they show up with legal people shoutin' for L&I. Yellin' they're sufferin' from emotional work stress. Most of 'em are fakin' it; the rest of us are on to 'em. This Karin, I agree," Mike mimics, 'Woops, I lost my crummy mind for a moment.' So then she gets off after killing someone and everybody is ready to jump to her bidding." Mike looks around the room for support. "You gonna buy this?"

Hanna swears, "It's the drugs. Drugs are a side effect of mental illness and makes things worse." She nods her head. "If this woman was black and from the south we wouldn't be sittin' here. She'd be convicted in a minute. But you take a white woman smokin' dope, who beats the livin' life out of somebody, and look at us here.

"They'se got us people here talkin' about this poor, poor woman, her mama didn't love her; the doctors … they argue amongst themselves for hours. Even got religious experts comin' in here arguin' about the facts they think they know about. Huh-uh, I tells you, I don't know if'n I should laugh or cry."

I protest. "What you said, Hanna, may be true, but does that make it right? We should just hurry up and give Karin a guilty vote, guilty of murder just because someone else wouldn't get a fair trial?"

"Yes, ma'am," Hanna shouts back in anger. "The law should be the same fer ev'ryone. But let me tell you somethin', little lady, it oughta be the same fer blacks as fer whites. It's the only way things'll ever change. But I don't 'spect you understand what I'm sayin'?"

I lash back. "I hear you saying that convicting Karin would be lousy justice. Is that what you just said?"

"No, you ain't got it, sister." Hanna flares. "Ah'm not sayin' that atall. What Ah'm sayin' is … a black woman would be convicted and that helps me make a decision to vote sane, guilty of murder, and I don't entertain no second thoughts 'bout it either. Her black hands atop the table are clasped so tight her knuckles show white.

Our heated arguments have exhausted us to the point that when the bailiff delivers our lunch, we eat in silence with little regard of each other or our surroundings.

During lunch my mind ponders. *Karin and my brother-in-law Mark have a lot in common. Their lifestyles may differ, yet they are the same. The morality for them is the same rhythm for all living people—happiness or pain. Their hopes, dreams, and aspirations for a decent life have been disturbed recently, and it's all pain.*

These two have been damaged physically and mentally. Demands were made of them and each met them the best way they could. Here I sit in this room confused, as is everyone around me. What are we doing here? Will this scenario be a repeat for Mark? What will we, the jury, be like after this trial is decided?

We jurors are told we have an obligation to decide Karin's fate. We weren't there. Something changed Karin and now I'm asked to sit in judgment of her.

I've no business being here; except, I now know something of what Mark faces and can only pray that his jury isn't as bullheaded as this one.

Tension in the room is unbearable as we resume afternoon deliberations. Everyone wants to be done with this trial. Time spent sitting in court has taken its toll on our nerves.

Dwayne and I view opposite of the others. They are hostages with our difference of opinion. I'm tempted to give in, but I've support from one other juror who agrees with me.

It's four o'clock, the day should be over. We've spent the entire afternoon in repetitious outbursts. There has been no headway or progress made for some time.

We sit in silent exhaustion when at a rap on the door, it opens and the bailiff sticks his head in to inquire, "Judge Daly wants to know if he should call it a day? He wants to know how ready you are to announce a verdict tonight? If not, we'll resume tomorrow morning."

I hear muttered protests and groans at the thought of repeating another day of jury duty. I know how they feel, they are weary in their efforts to convince Dwayne and me, of what they feel is misplaced concern.

They probably believe we are opposites just to be stubborn or perhaps that we enjoy an opportunity to hold authority over them. They exchange few words with us after it is decided to adjourn for the day.

On our way out we pass Judge Daly who scolds us for not coming to a decision. He reminds us of the cases yet to be tried and court time is valuable. Why are we dragging our feet? We arrived at the first verdict in just a short time.

~ ~ ~

I'm so drained and exhausted that during my ride home, I feel my last nerve fray. The kid sitting next to me has abrasive music blaring from his boom box ... a song rendition I recognize—*I'm A Believer*—by a group called the Monkees. My children know the words by heart and sing along with the recording. I'm familiar with *I Fought the Law*, but only the music and words, not the artist. If I have to concentrate anymore today, my reward will be a massive headache.

Pondering today's court proceedings, I conclude the army trains their troops to kill in war or get killed. While we jurors, void of any legal training, are thrown together to argue through our different opinions. It's best described as a room full of people speaking different languages trying to arrive at an agreeable conclusion.

I don't believe I've ever heard of a juror losing control and killing all their co-jurors. But there's always a first time and it wouldn't amaze me but that this could come about during my call for duty.

CHAPTER 18

I walk into bedlam; any thoughts pertaining to Karin Colby's trial will have to wait while I pass judgment on my home responsibility complaints.

Six children deluge me with assorted statements, questions and accusations. I find my way to the kitchen leading the Pied Piper way. I pick up as I go, straighten and hand off misplaced items to those behind me and dispense King Solomon's wisdom as we proceed.

From the chorus line I hear:

"Dad made chili, it's too hot a day to eat chili. Besides, we had it for lunch."

"Mom, testes are really balls, right? In health and PE they said—"

"You're late and I missed the bus for my piano lesson."

"Oh, Mom. Aunt Paula called and wants you to call her back."

"Mom, we're gonna be late for soccer practice."

And so it goes.

I rush to deliver one for her late music lesson and three fellows to the soccer field. I employ the oldest and the youngest to aid me in preparing a Kraft macaroni cheese dish. From my emergency provisions, I grab a box of frozen Banquet chicken and toss a salad of greens that have seen better days.

I leave supper to capable hands while I rush to retrieve everyone back into the fold. Supper greedily consumed, I stare at the table covered with dirty dishes. I'm exhausted. I have yet to do a load of laundry, lay out my clothes for tomorrow and sort through the mail.

I head for the kitchen with my hands full of dirty dishes when the phone rings. With skillful manipulation, I juggle the dishes and reach to answer.

"Jo?" My sister's voice comes over the line.

"Yeah," I say, "what's up?"

"Did Amy Sue tell you I called? Mark is really sick, an elevated temp, vomiting, and he's in a lot of pain with his back. He's weak as a wet dishrag. He's had this severe fatigue for some time, if you recall. I'm here at Madigan Hospital waiting for lab results and some other tests to come back."

"Need me?" I ask, hoping my voice doesn't convey my weariness.

"Mr. Dennis, Mark's attorney called. You're going to be served with deposition papers or did you get them in the mail today?"

"Papers? What's a deposition?" I croak.

"Mr. Dennis asks you questions about Mark and his habits; he needs to get a good profile of Mark as a family man and learn of any problems you know about for when he represents him in court."

"But, Paula, I'm biased. How can I help? I'm not through with jury duty. You can't ask me to help. It's too late; we're deciding the case tomorrow. Besides, what happens if I'm found out? I just haven't gotten around to telling the judge."

I endure Paula's long silent pause. "I don't know what to say, Jo," she says, "but you have to give a deposition or you can go to jail."

I explode. "For what, Paula? I haven't committed a crime, at least that I'm aware of. I didn't raise Mark. Ask his mother to represent him, ask the Army, they sent him home to us in this condition. I'm supposed to condemn him? For what, Paula?"

"Jo, I'm only telling you what Mr. Dennis told me to tell you. I didn't tell him about your being on jury duty. I only asked him what happens if someone refuses and if they have that right. He emphatically said, 'No'."

"Now just a minute, Paula. If a wife doesn't have to testify against her husband, what about family members? I'm prejudiced and I'm biased, Paula; I'm in favor of Mark. How can I be of service? Mr. Dennis will only waste his time and throw my deposition out."

"The other attorney is supposed to be there too, Jo."

"You mean to tell me they gang up on us? No, Paula, I'll go to jail and they'll have to let me take my kids with me. They don't pay jurors enough to try such a case. They would put my kids in foster homes like they did yours. I have always considered myself a law-abiding citizen … until now.

"Give me Mr. Dennis's phone number, Paula, I'm gonna call and ask him how I can be excused from giving a deposition. Maybe he'll think different after I tell him what I think of the court system."

"Don't, Jo. Let's work with this man. He's representing Mark and has his best interest at heart. Anything said to give Mark merit will only be appreciated by both Mark and me. Please, Jo."

I'm suddenly aware Paula is softly crying. "I miss my kids, Jo. I miss them so much. Please … will you help us? I have to go, they're bringing Mark back to his room. Bye for now." The phone goes dead.

Somehow the rest of the evening passes in a fog. Tomorrow, Friday, the court is usually closed, unless there is a case. And now … a deposition monster rears its head.

I need sleep, my head's about to explode with a tangled quandary of problems. Karin … I'd like to be sure Karin is guilty of insanity, but again she leans towards being sane.

Mark … I doubt he functions as a dutiful husband in his condition and he's accused of taking advantage of someone. *I don't know… I'm not sure of anything anymore.*

The minute Karin's trial is over, I'm going to pay little Kathy a visit and find out a few things on my own. I'll rehearse what to say and approach her by surprise. I don't dare accuse. I'll need to use discretion. No one must know. I'm not even going to share my plan with Glen.

I can't believe this Kathy is so wise to what she accused Mark of doing; surely, she isn't experienced. How did all this come about? Mark's story is he told her to leave and he thought she had gone.

Before dragging myself off to bed, I select the World Book Encyclopedia lettered 'L' and flip to the section on Law, run my fingers down till I come to the description of **Deposition: An out of court oral testimony that is used in written form later in court. An examination of a witness before the trial.**

So, evidence and witnesses are examined by the lawyers as to who and how they wish them shown at the trial.

A reference in my research lists the words *subpoena duces tecum,* **a Latin phrase meaning a subpoena for the production of evidence. Bring with you under penalty of punishment, books, papers, evidence for the court.**

One day at a time, I tell myself. Judge Daly wants the trial over, the jurors want the trial over, but no one seems to understand that Karin's life depends on how we vote. *The verdict of sanity or insanity has to be unanimous and there are two of us who still doubt. Where will it end?*

Waiting for sleep to overtake me, I rework my participation as a juror. It's not that I don't feel a responsibility for jury duty, it's the system that is unfair. I'm under enough stress with my home life. My life has nothing to do with Karin, but it's as if we—the jurors—are the ones upon whom this trial depends when really it should depend on those with whom she has contact. The guilt or innocence is the jury's responsibility? This is not true. It can't be.

I wouldn't want to be tried by Karin's peers. The system is defective. What about the protection and moral standards we jurors owe our families, our community? We can't possibly make a fair vote and please everyone, yet this is what is asked of us. What of the repercussions? Even the court implies ignorance of the law is no excuse. What an unfair disadvantage for jurors.

Karin is not a repeat violator, so what good then is it if we find her guilty or not? How can justice be served? We don't know if Karin will be helped by being found guilty of insanity. We don't even know the consequences if she's not guilty. Does the punishment fit the crime? What do we know?

What if we only make matters worse? Why participate in a system that is flawed, biased and harmful to another? Because I have to? This is unjust.

We jurors spend time arguing over facts and accounts as viewed from our beliefs and perspectives. Where in the Constitution does it say we are to try and if found insane, the party should be treated as a criminal? Jails, prisons ... these are the places to put people suffering from a mental disease? Surely not.

I'll do the best I can. Go with my gut reaction. How can I judge a dysfunctional, mentally disabled woman? I feel the wheels of what I judge uncertainty turning in my abused mind. I had no reason to doubt my ability to judge before I became a juror.

CHAPTER 19

Friday, the eleventh day, trial deliberations continue. This morning's weather isn't unusual for the month of June—a wet misty drizzle. The problem lies with school children who, after nine months of classroom confinement, dream of summer activities the minute schools are dismissed for summer vacations.

The scent from wet raincoats and umbrellas invades my express bus into Seattle. Attitudes are far from damp as we regulars greet each other verbally, or simply nod in silent acknowledgment.

Fellow jurors and I slowly climb the hill from the bus to the courthouse, our heads lowered against the light rain, not unlike those, I imagine, of a holy order, who pass each other silently.

On our entrance into the courtroom, the attorneys, Mr. Clemens beside Mr. Dowd, are both conversing quietly with little Emperor Daly attired in his regal black robe, sitting relaxed on his throne. The three nod and mumble acknowledgments as we make our way to the jury room.

Removing our coats, we quietly slide into our seats awaiting Dwayne Washington to chair the group. We aren't hostile to one another, just politely indifferent, each enveloped in our own personal opinion.

After yesterday, I consider changing my vote just to go along with everyone when a discussion arises between Mike and Ryan. There is a question concerning the Japanese psychiatrist, Mr. Toshi, a State witness.

"It's true," Ryan agrees, "I'll give him his due; he's eloquent all right, a no-nonsense type regular, but he grated on my ever lastin' nerves."

"I thought," said Mike, "he was stuck-up ... acted superior. I don't trust Japs. Never have since the war."

Mrs. Marshall in defense of what she previously stated, repeated, "I said, I thought he was too intellectual; he's too wise for his own good."

I felt a quietness about Mr. Toshi, an absence of aggression either in his voice or manner. I'm sure their dislike for Mr. Toshi stems from his use of the English language which is far better than most of the people in this room. He did use big words and he is a foreigner, an Oriental, so this makes him inferior in their judgment.

Mr. Toshi, Dwayne and I walk in parallel. *Dwayne and I are second-class citizens to ten people in this room. None of them hear anything we say. It's as I said before, 'We jurors lack the education for this duty.' We interpret words differently and we who disagree are foreigners, inferior in these other ten people's judgment. They can barely conceal their irritation at us for opposing them.*

I realize that to stick with our verdict, the trial will be over. It means the lawyers will have to start again, a new judge appointed, the case retried before another selected jury. All because Dwayne and I question our concerns over a woman who killed a man, and we don't believe she should be sentenced to jail.

I wonder if the expense of a new trial has crossed Dwayne's mind?

How little I know about mental hospitals. Would it really be any different than prison? The doctors stated that schizophrenia cannot be cured. Karin appears to be comfortable just the way she is, so maybe she wouldn't be helped by treatment. Does she even want help?

I examine a pencil just to keep busy. I really am not concerned with Karin's problems. I don't really care what happens to her. I'm not sympathetic. I'm sure she will never be productive and contribute to society. She will always be a burden to the taxpayers no matter how I vote.

This is an infuriating case. Karin took a man's life, yet she walks our earth and seeks justice as her salvation.

I can't imagine Karin and Mark in the same prison. Mark's life is worth saving in my estimation, over and above Karin. If the two were sent to a mental institution, I'd feel the same. Karin will survive in either, but Mark … Mark would die; it would be a form of suicide. Karin is here because she killed a man. Mark didn't.

Dwayne begins our day. "After we went home last night, I decided that if we returned this morning and still feel the same, as your spokesman, I have no choice other than to announce us a hung jury."

We voted again and less than an hour later the votes are a repeat. As declared when deliberations began today, Dwayne said, "I've no choice but to call the bailiff and have him tell the judge we're a hung jury."

At Judge Daly's request we file back into the courtroom and take our seats. Dwayne stands up to face the judge and announces, "We are deadlocked ten to two, Your Honor. It's a painful deliberation but we haven't moved anywhere in the last twenty-four hours."

A frustrated, exhausted courtroom erupts in pandemonium. People seek justice and it should be dealt with from the hands of those who know and are responsible for interpreting the law.

To me, Karin Colby's life is similar to a glass of water that tips and spills. It spreads and travels far beyond the Zen church or Mr. Nishimura's family. Karin leaves a trail of devastation and havoc. Society's focus is for us to repair her.

Looking out into the chaotic courtroom, I wonder if maybe Dwayne and I should have voted with the others to send her to jail. Society rules that people who hurt other people must be punished. The spilled water is easy to clean up and soon forgotten, but who heals the souls involved?

Again, I wonder, *Is this the right thing to do to satisfy a society that likes people punished for damage done to them. Is this right?*

The ten jurors are people with average ignorance of the law; they want an eye for an eye. But two of us don't agree with them that this is the right method.

I can't speak for Dwayne, but I'm unable to change my vote. I don't know what's right. I also don't know the consequences of either verdict. There's no other way, I believe, than the validity of my decision.

Mr. Nishimura's elderly sister cries and laments so loud, she is hastily removed from the courtroom by family members.

I'm sure we jurors thought when she left the room things would quiet down, but Judge Daly's repeated gavel pounding leaves little quietude. It comes as a surprise that our little Caesar isn't able to gain control.

Again Judge Daly stands at his throne, pounds his gavel and yells for quiet. His robe sleeves billowing out at his sides resemble a giant angry black hawk. Eventually he claims control of his courtroom.

Once his court is quiet and in order, he plunks himself down and stares at us. His eyes squinted into slits, his red face masks a frown. He opens his mouth and roars, "I refuse to accept your decision. This is a murder trial. Have you any idea how much it costs the courts to try a case? The witnesses, the lawyers, not to mention time and money. If *you* think I'm going to let you give up and go home after only twenty-four hours, you have another think a comin'. Back to the jury room." He gestures toward the door. "You will not return until you have fulfilled your obligation to serve justice with a unanimous verdict."

If we thought deliberations were bad before, we had no understanding of *bad* until we lived through what followed.

Stress mounted as deliberations continued. Poll after poll conducted showed no change whatsoever in votes counted. Opposing jurors made no effort to hide their exasperation. Discontent prevailed in the jury room at day end with still no verdict in sight.

A bone weary group was dismissed that night at the usual time and for the weekend but ordered back to jury duty the following Monday.

~ ~ ~

Monday morning, the twelfth day since opening arguments of the Karin Colby trial. Neither Dwayne nor I had a change of decision, nor did we the following day, Tuesday, the thirteenth day of the trial. I lost count of the deliberation time, but I was sure of one thing … one by one our fellow jurors abandoned any respect they may have had for us.

I grow frustrated and confused between the desire to change my vote and the fear that if I do then Dwayne will be alone, and it is a decision neither one of us want to live with for the rest of our lives. We firmly believe Karin Colby is out of her mind and we are doing the right thing by requesting Karin be sent to a mental institution.

The days and hours are beyond description, viscerally degrading. But Dwayne and I hold fast to our belief that sending Karin to jail is demoralizing. To punish her in this manner is not a responsible punishment for someone incapable of being responsible for their actions.

Sometimes I question, *What if Karin could have stopped herself?* But I'm never absolutely sure.

Dwayne reminded us, "In the United States, our law says everyone is innocent until proven guilty, and as a society, we must agree that it is better to let a hundred guilty souls go free than to send one innocent soul to jail."

His elbows propped on the table, his head between his hands, we hear him say, "If I were an innocent man wrongly accused of a crime, I would certainly hope at least one member of my jury would adhere to these values."

He raises his head to view those sitting at the table. "How can I change my vote? Is this what you're asking me to do, just to save taxpayers the expense of another trial? This should have no consideration or bearing on this case."

During my worst moments ... moments when I feel sure I'm going insane ... I'm reminded of my foster boys. They have lived through times far worse than this.

Every day they harbor blame for where they are because they believe they aren't good. Every day they live with the knowledge they are associated with parents who make bad choices and maybe the choices would have been different if they had been better kids.

They believe they suffer more harm to struggle and so they suffer the guilt of being sacrificed. I've heard them in times when they were despondent.

We decide to ask for transcripts of the testimonies and pore over the evidence. I'm sure most of us learned everything by heart, having gone over it so many times, again and again until memorized word for word.

We then decide the one quote from the American Bar Association report sums up the entire trial for us. '**There is no objective basis for distinguishing between offenders who were undeterrable and those who were deterred, between the impulse that is irresistible and the**

impulse not resisted, or between substantial impairment of capacity and some lesser impairment…'

We, the jury, are at last satisfied with our dilemma. We are in agreement that our unanswerable questions are answered at best by the quotation, **'Judge by moral guesses**.'

Ten people made the decision Karin Colby was deterrable. Dwayne and I guessed she was not. For days this same argument continued. Who is right and who is not?

Mary Alice rarely spoke to me during the arguments. I watch her click her tongue, close her eyes and then sigh as if she can't believe my interpretation.

Once, when I adamantly stated, "I don't believe it's possible for anyone to lose their mind. I don't believe anyone loses their mind on purpose. And besides, if it is possible, when are they aware they've lost their mind?"

I caught the look of disgust she shared with the others. I don't actually think she hates me, but from now on I'll make my way around her and I'm aware she and Laura Judson have formed a close friendship.

During a morning quick break, a saving grace for me comes when Grace admits her husband isn't the person she made the court think him to be. "He's a drunk, doesn't have a job, has been arrested and been in jail. She hadn't admitted this during the voir dire. Now she is terrified of being caught and having to pay a penalty. The only money they have to live on will be her jury money. She has to forfeit her pay to her employer in return for them excusing her to serve jury duty.

What a relief to know there is someone else who carries a fear of being caught and penalized as I would be should Mark's arrest be discovered. At Grace's confession, I fight the uncontrollable urge to give in to wailing and sobs. I bravely twist my face into a wobbly smile and pat Grace on the back. "Hey," I whisper, "this trial is almost over, Gracie, it's almost over."

I grab the moment to talk with Dwayne, alone, before everyone returns to their places.

"What do you think of the idea of going before Judge Daly and identify ourselves as the dissenters, Dwayne? And be willing to answer any questions the judge might put to us?"

Dwayne sent word by the bailiff to Judge Daly, who summons us into the courtroom. Dwayne explains for the second time, "We are a hung jury."

Once again the judge orders us back to the jury room, ignoring our request and without any comments or instructions.

We silently take our seats unsure of what to expect next.

CHAPTER 20

The late afternoon sun coming in through the bus window isn't enough to warm my soul. Fortunately I have a window seat and pretend to concentrate on the world outside rather than acknowledge the lady beside me. Bus seats are not designed for comfort. I'm sure it's to prevent people from falling asleep and missing their destination.

This morning after we met with Judge Daly and were sent back to the jury room, the bailiff entered to announce, "Judge Daly said he wants each of you to come before him—individually."

Dwayne elected to be first and returned after a few minutes. Linda was next, Harry followed, then Hanna. I'm eighth to be called.

I fight a terrifying thought, *The judge is going to trip me into giving away my innermost secret—how I'm not eligible to be on the jury.* I follow the bailiff into the courtroom where everyone present stares and scrutinizes me. The bailiff directs me to the nearest seat.

"Mrs. Simpson," Judge Daly's grave voice inquires, "what's going on in there?"

I panic, my stomach lurches, my throat is suddenly dry and I'm lightheaded, but I manage to keep calm and answer, "We seem to have reached an impasse, Your Honor."

"I'm aware of this." His piercing stare only unnerves me more. "What I ask and want to understand is, have the deliberations stopped entirely in there? Are you jurors even trying?"

"Yes, Your Honor, we've been deliberating the entire time."

"So, is there any chance you twelve will reach a verdict if you keep trying?"

I swallow to lubricate my dry throat. "I don't think so, sir."

"What do you mean, you don't think so? Mrs. Simpson, I don't intend to declare a mistrial if there is any chance that further deliberations will bring a verdict. I'm asking you … is there any chance a verdict can be reached?"

I shake my head. "No, Your Honor, I don't feel it's possible at this point."

I'm dismissed by little Caesar. Not only his voice, but his attitude irritates me. After my dismissal, I expect the entire courtroom to stand up and point thumbs-down in judgment of me as a juror. I meekly return to the jury room led by a silent bailiff.

Moments after the twelfth juror returns to the jury room, the bailiff summons us as a group to return to the courtroom. Starting with Dwayne, Judge Daly repeats the same question put to us individually.

"Mr. Washington, are you still willing to deliberate?"

Without displaying anxiety, I nervously wait for his answer.

Dwayne replied, "Yes, sir."

I breathe a sigh of relief. *Good, Dwayne, you are still with me, you're still holding out for a fair verdict.*

"Tell me," Judge Daly frowns. "Is there any chance, in your opinion, that further deliberations will result in a verdict?"

Dwayne pauses. "I don't believe there is, Your Honor."

Ryan's turn is next. He answers the judge as did Dwayne. "Your Highness, may I request permission to speak?"

I bite down on my lip to keep from giggling at the sight of Judge Daly's one lifted eyebrow. Ryan voiced my sentiment exactly … *your Highness. Perfect, Ryan.*

"Yes, and my position is referred to as Your Honor, not your Highness. Please, continue."

"Sorry, your High ... excuse me, I mean Your Honor. What I want to know is, when two of the jurors aren't willing to deliberate, what should we do?"

Judge Daly's face turns beet-red in rage. "It is against the law for a juror to refuse to deliberate. It doesn't happen in my court. We would have to start from the beginning again."

We watch his eyes narrow and his jaw clench. "I just asked each one of you if any of you refuse to deliberate."

He bellows at us. "If anyone of you jurors refuse to deliberate, you will be dismissed. I just asked each one of you, individually, and you each answered in the affirmative. I demand to know right now... what is going on here? Is someone not willing to deliberate? He pushes his black robe sleeves up the length of his short, hairy arms in a show of aggression. "I want to know."

Ryan glowers, leans forward and points first to Dwayne and then to me. I glance at the other jurors. Their eyes follow Ryan's aimed finger.

Judge Daly sits back on his throne and closes his eyes in meditation before he inquires in a placating voice, "Mr. Washington," he pulls his robe sleeves down, "is this true, you are no longer willing to deliberate?"

Everyone in the room is silent, every face is riveted on the two of us—the judge, the attorneys, the bailiff, reporters, visitors, the defendants and victim's families.

Though Dwayne is questioned first, I am suddenly emotionally devastated. I'm unprepared for any consequences. I begin to tremble. Being the focus of such strong disapproval coming from everyone creates an indescribable, lethal atmosphere in the courtroom.

I feel physically beaten, drained, ready to collapse. Then I look over at Karin. She isn't looking at us. Her eyes are closed and her lips are silently moving. Her lawyer Mr. Dowd is sitting back relaxed, following Dwayne's every word. He glances over to me while he doodles, unseeing, on a piece of paper atop his table.

His gesture captures my attention. Just then our glances meet and if I read his expression correctly, it's a combination of sincere respect and approval.

My panic subsides momentarily.

Looking beyond Karin and Mr. Dowd, I discern Mr. Clemens' frown. He's staring straight ahead at the wall behind Judge Daly.

Dwayne, slow to answer, tents his fingers before him and crosses one leg over the other. If he's nervous, it doesn't show; he is well composed.

"I'm not unwilling to deliberate, Your Honor; I think the problem is the other jurors are extremely agitated I don't share their opinion."

"Mr. Washington." Judge Daly appears interested in Dwayne's interpretation. "Are you honestly listening to their opinion?"

"Yes, of course, I am."

"And do you, sir ... Mr. Washington, honestly feel there is no chance of you changing your mind?"

"Your Honor, the deliberations have become repetitive, as I explained to you when you asked before. We are not getting anywhere. We continue to go over the issues again and again."

Judge Daly heaves a weary sigh and exchanges a glance with Mr. Clemens, the prosecutor. The judge then leans forward in his seat to address me.

"Mrs. Simpson." His voice conveys his fatigue. "Are you no longer willing to deliberate?"

"I've never indicated I was unwilling to deliberate, Your Honor." I begin to tremble again.

"What is your reasoning that the others feel you are unwilling to deliberate?"

"Your Honor." My voice quivers. "Mr. Washington states it well. I think my fellow jurors are just frustrated that I can't be convinced of their opinions."

"And do you honestly listen to their opinions, Mrs. Simpson?" The Judge rubs his forehead and passes his hand over his eyes before giving me his direct attention.

"Yes, I have, Your Honor."

"Then, Mrs. Simpson," Judge Daly inquires, looking straight at me. "You honestly believe there is no chance of you changing your mind either?"

"Your Honor, the disagreement with the others is over fundamentals ... not a disagreement over information."

Judge Daly is unable to hide his reaction of defeat. He had followed the legal procedure to its limits. We sit quietly awaiting his wrath at our judgment and his declaration of a failed verdict.

He focuses on the courtroom of silent viewers. "The jury, as you heard, has been polled. The court finds that further deliberation would be pointless and that this jury is hopelessly deadlocked. I, therefore, declare a mistrial. The jury is excused."

The sound of his gavel on the podium no longer carries authority. No longer does he appear the little Caesar I have envisioned him to be.

It's all over ... just like that ... the trial is over. I scan the room but only a few of Mr. Nishimura's family members remain in the gallery.

I glance over to Mr. Dowd. I really do not care for this man, but I'm sorry for him. He will now have to repeat the entire trial, or Karin may seek a new attorney.

Karin, sitting beside Mr. Dowd, smiles in the same pitiful manner she's displayed throughout the trial. I watch her mother reach over and awkwardly touch her on the shoulder. Karin doesn't appear to notice but looks over at the jury box instead. Our glances meet. I watch her shrug after a few seconds as if to say 'It wasn't a very happy ending.'

I was told earlier that after reaching a verdict, most jurors reconcile differences created from heated arguments, painful wounded feelings are set aside and they are able to generate a positive attitude towards each other.

Not so for us. Our jury botched the trial and everyone departs angry. I feel I have but two friends.

Dwayne, who maintained his dignity and accepted his responsibility throughout the highly emotional time. He was elected our foreman and during the worst of the deliberations, he remained polite to everyone. I imagine from his military background, he's learned to keep his head during impossibly stressful times and under extremely trying conditions.

And Grace, meek little Grace, so passive. A pitiful little woman with so few hopes and dreams. She is incapable of understanding anyone else's problems because hers are so great.

I remain in the courtroom until it has cleared. I don't care to meet up with any of the others. I'm extremely hurt concerning Mary Alice ... that she is not able to settle her differences. I didn't even see her leave the room. We exchanged phone numbers at the beginning of the trial to enable us to meet when it was over. I doubt she'll ever call me and I'm not sure of my feelings for her at this time.

I make my way through the courthouse and reach to open the door when a hand pushes it open for me. Dwayne startles me.

"Joella, I want you to know," we walk down the steps away from the building, "I understand how you felt during the trial. I didn't want you to leave without my good-bye." He held out his hand to me.

Mr. Dowd drew near from behind us. "I want to thank both of you. I've never had to go through what you just experienced. I'm not sure if I would be able to handle myself so courageously. It's been a difficult trial and even more difficult to understand. You two showed genuine concern under the most trying of circumstances. I applaud your judgment."

We three shake hands and Mr. Dowd swiftly turns and walks away before I can explain how much his show of appreciation means to Dwayne and me.

We jurors are not schooled in handling situations like we've just experienced. I will always feel it was Judge Daly's insensitive handling that brought about our insecurity to make a final decision. Neither lawyer will ever be able to take credit for their swaying the jury or their expertise in handling the case. I, as a juror, am here to confirm for the sake of argument, that juries are not qualified to judge in criminal issues.

The Supreme Court of the United States doesn't have to work with inexperienced jurors, they work out their differences between them. They are educated for the task. Jurors are not.

I dawdled so long, I missed my usual express bus. My call for duty has ended tragically. I'm downhearted.

Did we do our best? It remains to be seen how the next jury will handle Karin's case. How many times can a person be tried? Maybe she'll ask for a judge's decision. Is she allowed to do this?

Must Dwayne and I carry forever the guilt of how we two opposed, making a unanimous vote impossible? Perhaps Karin will break under all the stress and be confined to a mental institution? Who but God knows? Dwayne and I lacked the assurance that would have finalized the verdict. Is Karin sane or insane … will we ever know? She killed a man. However, in all fairness, do we convict a mentally sick woman for reason of insanity?

What is Judge Daly's concept of the mistrial? He would have been the one to make the final ruling as to the sentencing of Karin Colby. Will Karin's next prosecuting attorney and lawyer be as prudent as the team who served her?

I'm not free of the legal system. Mark, my brother-in-law, is next to face a trial. It will be interesting for me. I'm sure of Mark's innocence. There are extenuating circumstances that give me grounds to believe in his innocence. But, should his case go before a jury, I can't answer for the outcome.

CHAPTER 21

Immediately following the trial, Glen and I pack the family, including the dogs, for a camping trip to Denny Creek Campground at the foot of Snoqualmie Pass.

A sunny day with cotton-ball clouds floating in a blue sky just beyond the tips of enormous evergreens promises a great week for camping.

Glen and the boys pick a campsite close to necessities to pitch our tents facing away from the cook area wood smoke. The girls and I unload the camping gear.

Camp setup completed, the excited kids take off with our Westie dogs for their first hike up three mile trail to Franklin Falls. Glen and I relax in lawn chairs. We absorb the fragrance of cedars, the intoxicating odor of wood smoke, and fight off our persistent ravenous appetite until the kids return.

~ ~ ~

The week passes quickly with us back in town facing summer activities with trips to Tacoma to look in on Mark and visit Tammy and Jeff when it's convenient for their foster mother.

Still, there are nights when I suffer murder scene replays in my dreams. Vivid bitter memories remind me of how we were set up to fail. In their highly-competitive game to try cases, men and women with legal wisdom lose touch with the real world. They neglect responsibility, leaving the decision making to those of us less qualified.

Ordinary people, in general, rely on educated judges and lawyers for advice. We, as jurors, are at an unfair disadvantage. Not knowing the laws, we are forced to make a judgment with the results ending up as heavy weights on our conscience.

Justice in the hands of jurors means taking into account all the facts and rendering a fair judgment. However, relying on this belief, I was obliged to assess the trial with my opinion and in doing so, it severely affected my part in the deliberation.

We, as jurors, were never given a review of the legitimacy of the law. What if we had questioned the jury's right and duty to review these laws?

The first flaw was in accusing Karin of her violation of a law, regulation, or statute. And due to the nature of the trial, Judge Daly within his rights, chose to split the case into two parts. Murder and the sanity or insanity evidence only confused the issues for the jurors.

The second flaw: jurors need to be treated with respect. The system allows the courts to choose the jurors while the Constitution of the United States upholds the right of trial by one's peers. Here again, the system is dysfunctional by discrimination.

If there is a jury schooled in legal facts and terminology before a trial, I'm unaware. Do we jurors compromise one law to enforce another and does this resolve the situation? Jurors are not predestined students of law or we'd probably not be selected as jurors. Mr. Dowd had said as much.

~ ~ ~

The summer days pass swiftly with Mark's future of grave concern. We make the trip to Tacoma for our deposition hearing with Mark's attorney Mr. Dennis and Kathy's attorney Miss Lisa Spellman representing the Bishop family.

Miss Spellman questions our knowledge of Mark's alleged abuse to Miss Kathy Bishop. Before the deposition, Mr. Dennis suggested

Glen and I listen to the accusations against Mark and give only direct answers.

When it was our turn to speak, we painted Mark's background full of merit, up and beyond moral reproach, as the prejudiced family members we are. No trial date has been set at this time and Mark is free on his recognizance and with a medical disability.

I've decided, unknown to anyone, I will pay a visit to Kathy, the irresponsible teenager accusing Mark of sexual advancement charges.

During a visit with Paula, who has lost weight and is a bundle of nerves, I learn the doctors have informed her they discovered painful, growing tumors forming along Mark's spinal column. He too is losing weight, is irritable, and the once happy-go-lucky spunky Mark is emaciated, uncomfortable and weak. His bone leukemia is steadily progressing and giving him a great deal of pain for which he now relies on vast quantities of painkillers.

I hope it sounded casual when I stated, "I just became aware of how much teenagers spend at gathering hangouts. They must get huge allowances, from what the article described. It said shopping malls are a favorite place to meet. Do you happen to know the favorite hangout for like…say…Kathy and her friends?"

I watched Paula flinch at my question before she flares at me. "Jo, don't you dare get any ideas. Leave Kathy alone and don't mess up Mark's case. I respect Mr. Dennis's advice and I'd appreciate it if you and Glen would do the same."

In my best performance of feigning surprise, I ask, "Paula, are you accusing me? I simply asked if you happen to know the place because I recently heard how much money is poured into these teenage hangouts. Do you realize, you and I will soon be supporting these hangout places. I don't remember having time to hang out at such places when we grew up."

Paula appears astonished. "You don't remember the A&W drive-in? We little kids used to follow you, big sister; your group always knew all the fun places. You've forgotten the roller rink? How about the bowling alley? You've forgotten? Already suffering from a weak memory, huh? What a shame; you're still fairly young too."

I let her taunt me. It releases her mind from questioning me further and for a little while she is Paula, the sister I know.

The next week, I made an excuse to visit Mark during the afternoon when my kids have a swimming lesson. My friend Dorothy, whose children are the same ages as mine, will pick everyone up and take them to her house for ice cream until I get home.

I creep along in the heavy traffic from Seattle to Tacoma, headed to the hangout suggested by Paula.

I find a parking place at the I-Hop and enter the cool interior of the restaurant. First of all, I vaguely know what Kathy looks like from the few times when she'd come to babysit at Paula's. Second, I didn't dare approach her with accusations. I gaze around to see young people assembled in nearby booths and didn't spot her.

A young tired appearing waitress with menu in hand comes to seat me. "I'm looking for someone, may I check to see if they are here yet?" She steps aside allowing me to proceed down and around the U-shaped aisle with booths on both sides.

I had just rounded the turn where a large oversize booth is filled with laughing, loud-talking teenagers. One of them facing me I identify as Kathy.

Her bleached blonde hair is done up in the typical pompadour fashion of the times. Her eyelids heavy with thick mascara lashes barely hold open her usually large brown eyes. Her dramatic gestures fascinate the mixed gender group similar in age to her, who howl hilariously at something she said. She doesn't appear aware of me passing their table.

It would be a wrong move to draw attention to myself or her, so I make my way to the front and wait to the side while an elderly couple settle their bill.

The weary, young waitress is nowhere in sight. Wanting to remain incognito, I wait patiently for the cashier to acknowledge me.

The hostess seats me in another section of the restaurant, away from Kathy, with many windows exposing the parking lot perfectly. I order coffee and ice cream to bide my time. My hopes are to catch Kathy alone, but it appears impossible this first visit. At least I know she hangs out where Paula suggested. Now, to get her alone.

Presently the group breaks up. I pray Kathy might lag behind. From my window I watch her and two other girls leave and make their way north to the intersection.

Hastily I pay the cashier and make a mad dash outside, but the girls have vanished. Once inside my car, I decide to drive north for several blocks taking a different route to where they were headed. I drive down the long city block then turn right to maybe catch a glimpse of them.

I round a corner several blocks from I-Hop and would have made a free right turn but oncoming traffic makes it impossible. Just then, Kathy and her friends approach the intersection; with the light in their favor they cross in front of me.

My mission concerning Kathy is so near and yet so far away. I turn the corner and head for the freeway. Today is not the time, but at least I know where she and her friends gather.

I keep to my daily routine and am able to wait up for Glen at night. I set his plate of food before him and take a chair to keep him company while we discuss daily issues.

I don't dare, but wish I could share with Glen my adventure today. I listen to his account of "Two young hippies came in today. They were driving an old minivan, wearing those tie-dyed T-shirts and faded worn-out blue jeans. They wanted to know about ordering supplies. Hard to imagine them owning a computer business—Micro-something or other. These kids and their wild ideas; hard to believe they will ever amount to anything. But they seem to know their business, just not how to dress. And that long-hair makes 'em appear even more radical."

To show interest, I inquire, "Fellows from around here, you think?"

"Yeah, I remember their first names because they were such common names—Bill and Paul. Think one of 'em said his last name was Gates. I only overheard a little of what they said. Bob was taking care of them."

The next day Paula's call was encouraging but on the other hand depressing. "Mr. Dennis phoned," she explained. "He doesn't understand why, with Mark an invalid, Tammy and Jeff can't come home. Mark will have to be served with restraining orders, but he isn't likely to be coming home in his condition anytime soon.

"Mr. Dennis says that with the State screaming for budget cuts ... why leave Tammy and Jeff on the welfare rolls?"

I praised Mr. Dennis's wise decision but didn't mention my concern for Mark. "I'll come help you collect the kids, Paula, soon as they can make the move.

"You have to appear in juvenile court first," I tell her. "That means caseworkers come to approve the house, your working hours, who you get for child care, your budget and ... oh, don't worry, it goes fast once you get started. Is Mr. Dennis representing Mark in family court or do we need to request another legal assistant?"

Hearing the excitement in Paula's voice, I am energized.

"I think Mr. Dennis is going to represent Mark. I just can't think fast enough, Jo. I'm so excited."

"It's not done overnight, Paula, but I'll help in anyway I can. Let me suggest you make a list and put Mr. Dennis first. Ask if he will represent you. If not, we need to know so we can get you a counselor. You sound so excited."

I feel my depressed spirit lift after her call. I once again feel a surge of vigor course through my veins—the quality of life I had enjoyed and taken for granted before the days I served on the disastrous hung jury panel. My confidence soars, my self-worth returns in the wake of Paula's jubilation so evident in her phone call.

Hanging up the phone, I find myself standing in a path of vibrant sunlight streaming through the kitchen window. I silently mime a thumbs-up.

CHAPTER 22

I rehearse what I'll say to Kathy Bishop as I weave in and out of traffic headed for Tacoma and I-Hop, the local teenage hangout. I wonder what attracts the teenagers to this place? It's a quiet family-style restaurant; no blaring jukebox music for one thing. What is there about it that draws the younger crowd?

I have a choice for parking today; a sign the restaurant is doing little business this Thursday afternoon.

I recognize the waitress from my previous visit. She greets me with the same bored expression. A few strands of brown hair have escaped the confines of her carelessly trussed hairdo to loosely frame her face and soften her sharp features.

Quickly I scan the room and there, seated with a girl her age, is Kathy. "Please, just a cup of coffee." I indicate a booth. "I see my party seated right over there."

My throat dry, my tongue stuck to the roof of my mouth, I slide in beside Mark's nemesis. "Hi, Kathy." I feign familiarity. "I stop here sometimes on my way home from visiting Mark, before hitting that ghastly traffic back to Bellevue. You remember me?"

I'm greeted with a vacant stare.

"Should I?" she sarcastically retorts and lowers her heavy mascara-coated lashes. She doesn't appear startled by my invasion, merely uninterested.

"Kathy, I'm Jeff and Tammy's Auntie Jo. Remember?"

"So? …Why should I care?"

Kathy's testy manner gives her girlfriend reason to look silently from one to the other of us in puzzled interest.

Where do I begin? I rehearsed my lines…but now I can't remember how it's supposed to go, nor how I planned to lead off the conversation.

The waitress sets a coffee carafe before me with a white pottery coffee cup and asks, "Will there be anything else?" Her mundane attitude fits her manner.

Kathy attempts to exit the booth but is unable to get out with me next to her.

Next, she makes a desperate plea to her girlfriend, "Let's go. C'mon, Linda, I gotta go." She expects me to move so she can leave.

I don't budge and seize the moment. "Kathy, before you leave, may I ask you a couple of questions?" *I have her caged in and she knows it.*

"Either of you care for coffee?" I invite, holding the carafe out to them. "Or, how about a refill on cokes?"

Kathy's temper flares. "I don't really have anything to say to you, whoever you say you are."

Her bewildered girlfriend, across the table, stares intently, first at Kathy then at me.

I have to talk fast. I'm not experienced to handle a situation like this.

"Kathy, I'm here because … to apologize for my brother-in-law Mark attacking you. Kathy…Mark is dying." I don't allow myself to catch my breath. "He's been a sick man for a long time. You know this, of course. I don't want him to die leaving behind a bad image for his wife and children, nor for his family and friends."

Kathy makes another attempt, maneuvering to get me to move. "Linda, come on. Let's go."

I refuse to budge and turn to Kathy's friend. "Linda, will you help me? I'm sure you've heard about Kathy's charge against Mark. I can't let Mark die and have his children think their daddy is an evil person. Does this make sense to you? Will you help me convince Kathy how serious her accusation is?"

There, I said it. I'll probably go to jail for confronting Kathy, but I can only hope she will confess that she lied about Mark. Why didn't I think to bring something to write on and have her sign or a recorder to tape our conversation. I'll make her words stick somehow, that is... if I can get her to admit her story isn't true.

Linda, thoroughly confused, shrugs and stutters she knows little about the circumstances.

I mutely disagree. *Girlfriends, especially close girlfriends share secrets. I remember my girlfriends and we had secrets. Times are no different.*

Linda, a tiny trim girl remains seated. "I don't know you and besides, Kathy is my friend. Why would you ask this of me?"

I turn to Kathy. She's anxious, awkwardly raised from the seat, hands on the table ready to take flight but still unable to get past me.

"Don't you say a word, Linda, or I promise you, our friendship is ended."

"Kathy, when I was your age ..." I challenge the two. "I didn't really know what rape meant. Are you sure you understand what the word implies?"

Kathy scowls, sits down, inches over to the far side of the booth, crosses her arms and snaps defensively, "I'm not supposed to talk about this. You're asking me to break the law. Besides, it's none of your business." She pauses a few seconds then accuses, "You came here on purpose didn't you? You came here to scare me into telling you something."

Our energized waitress approaches the table with a surprising vitality I'd not viewed in her before. "I'm off in a few." Even her voice is friendlier. "I need to clear up loose ends before I leave ... are you about finished here?"

The bill I grab from my purse and hand her would cover far more than a couple cups of coffee but worth it if I can get Kathy to tell me why she's accusing Mark.

We three sit silent, Kathy glaring at me. *How can I make this girl talk? I'm sure by the way she acts, she has lied about the whole affair and now caught in her lie is afraid. But how to make her own up to her finger-pointing?*

"Kathy, I know this is difficult for you, and I'm repeating myself, but Mark may not live long enough for the trial. He's sick. Please, will you reconsider what you told your folks and the cops? Just a different choice of word can make a difference in his life.

"Of course, if he did take advantage of you, you need to defend yourself. But if ... if there is a chance you might have used the wrong word or misunderstood what rape means. You don't have to explain to me, but will you talk this over with your folks and your attorney, or your friend Linda here?"

I pause in hopes she will consider my request. "I'm pleading for Mark, Kathy. Neither he nor Paula know I'm here. Mark's dying and you have a whole lifetime ahead of you. If it's possible you can clear his name before he dies, there are many of us who will be forever grateful to you."

I toy with the cup handle to keep from facing her silent hostility.

Linda finally speaks up to ask, "Kathy, what really did happen to you?"

I remain quiet while the two converse. Linda's question seems to affect Kathy more than anything I've said.

It's my turn to look from one girl to the other when Linda says, "Kathy, I don't remember you coming right out and saying he had sex with you. Did he?"

Kathy picks at the polish on her thumbnail before she answers, "No, it didn't go that far."

I don't interrupt when Linda inquires into Kathy's story.

"You didn't tell me he touched your privates. I thought you said he only kissed you. Isn't that what you said?"

I don't dare move. Linda's interrogation is better than any questions I've posed so far.

Kathy's answer is barely audible. "My dad is the one who got carried away. When I told my mom I wasn't going to babysit there anymore and the reason, she told my dad and he threatened to go over there and blow Mark away. I didn't mean for it to get out of hand."

I silently watch Kathy aggressively wipe tears from her eyes. "My folks are always nagging me to get a job. I don't like being around Mark. He's sick all the time and he says mean things to everyone. He even yelled at me a few times. I don't like him."

We three are silent after Kathy's confession.

On the verge of tears, I instruct, "Kathy, we have to tell someone. You are right; this has been blown out of proportion." I hurry on, "Your dad feels protective of you, Kathy, you're his daughter. He loves you, his actions are understandable. I had a feeling this wasn't as bad as everyone made it out to be. Don't be scared; just tell your attorney your story as you've told Linda and me."

Suddenly realizing I have advantage of the situation, I continue, "Kathy, we must help Mark. Tammy is about to lose her protector, her dad who loves her as much as your daddy loves you. When her daddy dies, she won't have anyone to stand up for her. Can you understand why I want to help Tammy's dad? He's been charged with doing something really bad. He needs absolved of this untrue accusation. Will you do this for little Tammy?"

Kathy, her head bowed, nods in the affirmative to my plea.

I offer the girls a ride home, but Kathy declines saying she'd rather walk. I head for my car feeling a sense of relief that my guilty deed has paid off by Kathy confessing Mark never touched her in the way she had claimed.

It isn't until I'm on the way home that I realize Kathy told me one thing but she well might deny it later. And Linda, being her good friend will support Kathy.

I don't have verification that any of this took place. Where do I go from here? If I contact Mr. Dennis then he'll know I'm messing in affairs that are none of my business. What right did I have to question her? Paula, Glen, everyone is going to be upset with me, and what have I managed to accomplish? Nothing said today has established facts. Then my mission failed … nothing I did will be of help to Mark.

Later that evening, I drag myself to the boys' soccer game. Seated in the bleachers with friends and neighbors, my mind is not on the game. A heavy weight has settled in my heart of how I messed up this afternoon.

Our foster son, Jay, is a born athlete; his skill shows in his ability to maneuver himself. The crowd watches his agility and command as he dribbles the ball down the field. His precision technique, with teammates in close pursuit keeping the opposing team from closing in and capturing the ball, is like a choreographed performance. Time and again I've watched the boys work. They are a united team. To view them in action is to watch perfection.

I'm aware from the crowd's reaction that Jay and the team are functioning as the well-trained team players they are. However, lost in my thought of Kathy and Linda, I'm not concentrating on the game.

Afterwards, I'm given a play by play account of how the opposing team closed in just as Jay kicked the ball to my son Grant, who anticipated the move. Grant was to receive the ball and kick it beyond reach of the goalie poised ready for the ball to keep it away from inside the goal territory.

An opposing team member suddenly seeing an opening made a daring move and kicked the ball downfield out of the goalie's range. My son rushed in; using his head he bunted the midair ball turning its aim back towards the goal line. Bill, our other foster son, raced in to receive the ball and as it dropped, he kicked sending it above and beyond the uplifted hands of the goalie waiting to ward it off.

The "Jet" supporters jump and scream in delight. Lost in thought, the play that gave us the winning score of the evening eluded me.

I feel worse than ever. I failed at my attempt to help Mark and missed witnessing the teamwork between my boys that brought them victory.

Much to their outward demonstration of disgust, I smother my gladiators with affection and sing their praise in front of adoring fans.

How proud Glen will be to hear their recount of the game. I remember his prediction after a few of their games. "We're headed for State; I better get myself some time off to be there for the fellows when they play."

I wish I could bare my soul to Glen concerning what happened today between Kathy, Linda and me. I wish I knew where to turn, what step to take next. Who will accept the hearsay evidence of my conversation with Kathy this afternoon? Can I depend on her to tell someone besides Linda and me? Will someone listen to her?

Lying in the still warm darkness of night, I hear Glen beside me breathe in his soft rhythmic tempo. The crickets chirp noisily outside the open bedroom window. I hear the breeze softly rustle the branches of the big evergreens. I'm unable to sleep.

Mark dear, I opened Pandora's box today. I did it on purpose; I did it for your sake. What have I done?

CHAPTER 23

The date is September of 1992, my jury summons arrived by mail, as did my first in 1972. My commute will be a duplicate of yesteryear with commuters racing for seats on the early morning expresses into town and with a return scenario repeated each night.

Over the years, the bus routes have changed. They now travel through an underground tunnel emerging onto the I-90 floating bridge without a center bulge. The bridge once meant negotiating curves around the center draw span that allowed boat passage to either end of Lake Washington. Boats now pass under the bridge at the high end.

Seattleites take advantage of Lake Washington for fishing, water skiing and pleasure craft. The first weekend in August is set aside for the unlimited hydroplane races along with the breathtaking *Blue Angels*, a Navy precision flying group.

From across the United States, the big hydroplanes come to compete with local drivers. The boats too have progressed through the years from propeller-driven to jet power that propels the *hydros* around the blue lake water race course at great speeds sending white-water rooster tail plumes higher than their granddaddies before them, and at times literally take flight.

~ ~ ~

Today the new courthouse is a bluish-glass structure held together with metal beams and flanked by other skyscrapers on the Seattle skyline.

The windowless courtrooms have given way to spacious floor to ceiling windows. Gone are the artificially lighted, claustrophobic rooms.

Through the afternoon traffic headed for Bellevue, my mind calls forth memories of my first jury summons. The large, drab jury pool waiting room filled with metal folding chairs, a wooden table laden with packets of coffee, tea and cocoa beside a hot water dispenser. A short movie still delivers information for new potential jurors concerning their patriotic duty, and ancient, dog-eared periodicals are still strewed about.

I find today's prospective jurors friendlier, or perhaps I know what to expect. Jury selection still weighs heavy, time-wise, for idle hands awaiting their call to serve.

Before entering the jury pool holding room, we trade our summons for a name tag and accept script for our travel fare.

I settle in a middle chair between a man and woman and comment on changes I'm noticing in the room since serving in 1972. Each admits they served previously and agree they are aware of revisions in furniture and décor.

To my left, the man's name tag reads Bob Jacky. He's a tall, slender, chemical engineer; his bright blue Levi's and a sports jacket seem inappropriate—one of the accepted changes of the time. He's younger than me and the lady to my right.

With little encouragement he furnishes a full account of his last session. Then one leg positioned over the other, he fingers the name tag attached to his jacket pocket as he emphatically states, "What a privilege for me to serve jury duty again. A real privilege to be chosen. My patriotic duty; I'm glad to serve."

I can't help but wonder how this man would feel if he'd served on a hung jury as I had. The letdown after what I considered was my duty ... my responsibility. But due to my fundamental belief and inexperienced judgment, along with Dwayne Washington, we failed our patriotic duty. Hardly a privilege.

The lady beside me rapidly blinks her eyes, a habit prone to contact wearers. Her name tag reads Karen Ortlie. "I had to be excused from work again," she grumbles. "I already served on jury duty several years ago. Can't say much has changed. It surprises me more attention isn't paid to us jurors."

Her complaints stem from insufficient pay and lack of secure locker or storage for her personal items. "Ain't no place atall ta put purses, lunches or hang our coats. I don't understand why the same people are always summoned for jury duty. What about the rest of them tax-paying citizens out there? Some people tell me they's never had a summons."

"My only gripe," Bob comments, "is I didn't particularly like them collecting our notes at the end of the day. I would have liked to review them later that night."

"Notes?" I question in astonishment. "You took notes?"

"Ya has ta," Karen said. "How else ya gonna 'member the more 'portant and special issues?"

"Things have definitely changed from when I last served," I tell them. "We weren't allowed to question or take notes while the trial was being heard. It was a rather difficult situation for those of us who knew nothing concerning the interpretation of legal issues."

Bob chuckles and asks, "Were you reminded that you better not be caught talking to a fellow juror outside the jury room?" He swiped a hand across his neck to indicate the consequence at being apprehended talking to another juror outside the court boundary.

"Oh, we didn't ask questions," he admits. "I know it takes time to clarify some of the issues … so if it takes precious court time, I figure so what? It's the court's job to make it lucid enough for me to understand or I'm not making a decision one way or the other."

His attitude reminds me of Ryan, another opinionated juror during my jury duty of Karin Colby's disastrous trial.

A silence follows until I state, "I don't care for how the courts discriminate. They use the word *peer* and to me this means you are in someway acquainted with the lifestyle of the accused.

"Are you aware that in reality, the attorneys pick jurors they want, even over and above the one on trial might suggest. The formality of allowing the accused to pick a juror is granted only as a polite gesture by our legal system."

Karen cocks her head to read my name tag. "Joella, I agree. Last time I was picked, and for the life of me I sure never knowed why, it was ta serve on a drug case. The accused shot his best friend. A family man I might add, a man he thought had squealed on him. The case was surely an eye-opener for me, you better believe. I had no idea people lived such dangerous lives. Sure was different from the way I was growed up."

A trim lady in a brown uniform interrupts our conversation to request attention. She then reads twenty-five names from a list and directs all to follow the bailiff. My name is one of those read.

Bob and Karen both wish me luck as I excuse myself to join the others. The movie instructions state we aren't compensated the ten dollars a day allotted, unless we're hearing a case.

The bailiff leads those of us called into a wide open courtroom with light colored vertical blinds at the windows. The room is furnished with modern molded metal furniture. The gallery section blue padded chairs look inviting over the wooden benches of my past and the jurors' section has individual swivel chairs.

After settling ourselves, a youthful gentleman already seated at the podium greets us with a pleasant smile and introduces himself as Judge Patrick McKenna.

He then introduces us to Mr. Dumont, the King County Prosecuting Attorney, and Mr. Dumont's assistant. They occupy one of the two metal tables in front of us. At the other table to our right is the Defense Attorney, Miss Turner, who stands to greet us and gives me the impression she's an uncompromising, strictly professional young woman. Her dark-blue tailored suit fits what I'm positive is a diet regimented body void of jewelry. Her dark hair severely pulled back outlines soft feminine features, making her age difficult to estimate.

Beside her is a grossly obese woman in worn, faded, blue jeans and bright multicolored smock top. As she half turns, I'm astonished to look into a pale, haggard teenager face framed by long stringy hair and no makeup. Her round-shouldered dowager's hump gives her a tired, weary and aged appearance for one so young.

Judge McKenna then describes the case. "Miss Christina Maria Daniels is a fifteen-year-old girl who is found to have self-delivered an infant. The fully developed, full term body of a newborn boy with placenta still attached was found wrapped in a common terrycloth bath towel by a janitor dumping garbage into an apartment house disposal receptacle on March first of nineteen ninety-one.

"The janitor, on discovering the infant, notified the Seattle Police Department. According to procedure, the infant's body was turned over to the King County Coroner.

"Sometime later, Miss Daniels sought emergency treatment at Harborview Medical Center for excessive vaginal bleeding. Doctors treating her determined her condition resulted from a recent birth but Miss Daniels had come in without an infant and denies birthing a baby.

"Miss Daniels' vaginal tissue biopsy, obtained from the doctors at Harborview, was sent to the histology lab for analysis. At the same time, with no knowledge of Miss Daniels or the baby being related, a blood sample from the expired infant's umbilical cord was obtained. The histology and hematology technicians working from samples discovered a tissue and blood cell match; Miss Daniels' and the infant's were compatible. The blood match along with documented time coincide that Miss Daniels is the alleged mother of the infant she denies she birthed and abandoned.

"The Seattle Police were notified. With a court order Miss Daniels was placed under arrest and after medical treatment she was booked into the King County Juvenile Detention Center.

"She is pleading not guilty. Whether intentional or not, you, the jury, upon hearing all evidence and facts, will be asked to decide if Miss Daniels is guilty of malice of forethought, which is first degree murder or guilty for reason of insanity."

Here we go again, I thought. *How is it possible for us to judge her sane or insane? The act was insane, but...she had murdered her helpless, newborn baby.*

Judge McKenna requested jury selection proceed. He first heard excuses for hardships jury duty might cause members and declined or narrowed the excuses with graciousness, dignity and a sense of humor.

I decided when I first received my summons that I had no intention of repeating the trauma I'd endured from my first experience. I also felt more self-assured, as a citizen to defend my fundamental principles.

Judge McKenna requested the bailiff give us a break before jury selection. It surprised me we weren't ordered to stand while Judge McKenna departed the room.

When court resumed, the legal team ordered the prospective jurors be called by last names. Each time a person was expelled or selected, those already assembled in alphabetical order had to reseat themselves. Most of those on the list had been interrogated before my name was called.

When my turn came for interrogation, I stated my name and began immediately by listing my fundamental biases. "I'm for the death penalty; I want laws for stronger penalties in domestic violence cases; I'm for abortion and I do not condone court leniency. And I even quoted from a slogan I'd heard somewhere, "You do the crime, you serve the time."

The courtroom had been quiet during the questioning by the legal teams, but with my sudden declaration, a silence—a stillness so profound—settled over all. I felt as though time had stopped and remained so until Judge McKenna cleared his throat. Clasping his hands atop his desk, he stared so piercingly, I was sure he could see me break into a cold sweat and tremble.

"Let me ask you, Mrs. Simpson. If this were you in the place of this young woman … would you not want a jury to hear your case?"

I didn't have time to respond before he asked, "Do you mean to tell me," he paused, "are you telling us you're not willing to deliberate with an open mind? Your mind is so rigid you're unable to hear both sides of this case?"

"Your Honor, Judge McKenna, this is the first time the court has inquired of my principles and fundamental beliefs. I beg the court's indulgence to respect me as an American citizen. I have no intention of changing, excusing or altering my ideals—my right as stated in the Constitution of the United States. Yes, I am a prejudiced juror."

Judge McKenna exchanged looks with the two lawyers, scrunched up his mouth into a pout and frowned at me. "You realize … Mrs. Simpson, we have an obligation as American citizens. The court is only asking you as a juror to have an open-mind … to accept your duty to deliberate on jury duty. Do I hear you saying you refuse to deliberate?" He pauses momentarily as though waiting for me to change my mind.

I feel all eyes in the room staring at me, and I'm unable to control my trembling. "May I remind Your Honor, even in the military, citizens with fundamental beliefs and principles are allowed rights as conscientious objectors?"

Judge McKenna remains silent. A stern expression and glare gives me to understand his disgust with being challenged. Turning to the lawyers he asks "Counselors, how say you? Do you wish to challenge this juror?"

Mr. Dumont and Miss Turner approve my removal. Judge McKenna excuses me.

I pick up my purse and upon leaving the courtroom, I hear him say, "Please proceed with jury selection." It was as if I had never existed.

I have to admit I was curious about the young Christina Daniels case and hope the jurors will be lenient with her, but … she, like Karin Colby, took a life and to me this is insanity and our courts are not educated to measure the thin line between sanity and insanity. Therefore, I don't wish to aid or abet any part of an inept legal system.

Returning to Bellevue's Park and Ride, I pause inside my car to enjoy the sunshine on this warm fall day with the world blazing in brilliant colors. I watch others drive out of the parking lot. I'm not ready to leave yet.

I'm remembering a trial that took place in 1974. My heart and soul are with Mark.

His life on earth ended much too soon. Bittersweet memories are all that remain for our families.

~ ~ ~

The day of his trial was a beautiful fall day, much like today. The courts try few cases during the summer months in order for members of the legal system to enjoy extended vacations with their families.

Mark, to me, was a priority. He was dying and my fear was that we wouldn't get a court date in time.

Due to his declining condition, Mark would never have been able to withstand a later trial. And so when court finally convened, Mr. Dennis, knowing Mark's condition, suggested to everyone involved that due to the defendant's health limitations we consider a non-jury trial, even though it was an unusual request.

I carried in my heart the hopes that Kathy would speak out and confess to her wrong accusation, but I also knew she was afraid of her dad and what would happen to her if she were to recant her accusation.

Under extreme anxiety and against all ethics, I broke down and called Mr. Dennis, who admitted his suspicion of Kathy's unreliability.

"If we can request a non-jury trial, we won't need evidence as in a jury trial to establish him incapable of having assaulted Kathy; however," he added, "you must understand, Kathy's defense is working on her behalf and her parents are angry."

My life was a turmoil. I didn't dare tell my family that Mr. Dennis agreed with me that Kathy wasn't being honest, nor his suggestion to have a non-jury trial.

Then, one morning Paula called, "Mr. Dennis says he talked with Miss Spellman and she talked to the Bishops. They agree with Mark so sick, we should consider the probability of a non-jury trial. But, Joella, I'm not in agreement."

My sister is livid with rage. "Mr. Dennis is telling me that he talked this over with the other lawyer and those Bishops *first* ... not me. And he says a judge set trial is less formal than a jury trial. The judge is not held to a strict ad ... oh, whatever the word is of courtroom procedures with rules and rules of evid—"

"Paula," I interrupted, "what a great idea; this way, we don't have to drag Mark into court and the word you're looking for is *adherence*. It means the judge doesn't have be as strict as in a jury trial. He's able to accept the facts at hand.

"You know, Paula, if he has any doubt concerning evidence, he's more apt to request better findings than a jury gets. Believe me, I know this."

In other words, I'm thinking, there will be none of the inflammatory, irrelevant or otherwise inadmissible evidence that I'd been influenced by in the Karin Colby trial.

Paula wailed, "A jury would be more sympathetic than a lone judge, especially women jurors. I don't know ... I just don't know what to say, Jo. It's like everyone is agreeing to something I don't even understand. I don't like how this is going."

I patiently work to convince her that lawyers choose a jury to make their case. "It's taking a chance, sure. But Paula, look at it this way. Because of Kathy's age, the jury might make Mark out to be deranged due to his illness. A jury might sympathize with her."

Paula admitted, "Yes, and Mr. Dennis did say, 'There is never an assurance in requesting a non-jury trial that either Mark or the Bishops won't change their minds and request a jury trial.' We always have the right to appeal."

I implored Paula. "Mr. Dennis is a wise man, you said so yourself. I honestly believe our chances for Mark, in his condition, are far better with a judge ruling. A judge is experienced in dealing with a case of this nature. Paula, I'm almost positive he'll absolve Mark of the charges."

This isn't the time to tell Paula that Mr. Dennis and I feel Kathy isn't telling the truth.

It came to me suddenly that day ... *I had allowed myself to get caught up in circumstances and emotions that were none of my business. I hadn't even researched the facts that might have helped Paula understand better ... the percentage of convictions by judges over jury trials. Why didn't I have more facts to present to my sister? Besides, this is between Paula and her husband.* I had to bow out. It was their decision to make ... a judge or jury trial.

How useless I felt that day. I could only pray that Paula would accept the fact that Mark was unable to make a reasonable decision and the trial rested with her. I could only hope she would make up her mind in time to clear Mark's name for his family.

I inserted the key in the ignition. *I knew I wouldn't be accepted for jury duty today. I know deep down in my heart, I simply didn't want to experience feeling the responsibility or that part of my past repeated. I understood the fears my sister had concerning Mark, dear lovable Mark, who left us far too soon.* The circumstances of choice were beyond her limit of knowledge but became her responsibility.

She told me later she could only hope that God and Mark forgave her hesitation to make a decision.

CHAPTER 24

My garden is alive with sounds. A gentle breeze rustles the shrubs and tree leaves, bees hum their monotonous tune while they search flowers for nectar, birds gossip to one another and some bravely dip in the birdbath—all tolerant of my being nearby basking in the warm afternoon sunlight.

This type of day transitions me back to nineteen seventy-four ... a similar time of year. It was September, the court date to try the case of my brother-in-law Mark, accused of assaulting young Kathy Bishop, the fifteen-year-old babysitter.

I have since forgiven my sister Paula. She can be so exasperating at times. Their attorney, Mr. Dennis—what a jewel he was. Knowing Mark's time here on earth was limited, he worked quickly for a non-jury trial—one tried by a judge.

Paula should have been grateful, but no, she wanted a jury. The family tried to convince her, for Mark's sake, that it would be faster and a judge more professional to hear the evidence than a jury. I knew and spoke from my experience and involvement of the jury system, which I will always feel is a breakdown of the American legal system.

Mark, up until his health declined, was a handsome, rugged, outdoorsman ... a farm boy full of life and dreams. He completed his

Marine service in Vietnam. His letters home to Paula, shared with me, were filled with an intense longing to get home, pick up his life again and start a family. But again, his future with the Marines was tempting with benefits for his family and an early retirement.

He adored Tamara, his first born, but he was ecstatic over baby Jeff, an answer to his prayers. A son to carry on his name, fish and hunt with him and watch the Dodgers beat the Yankees.

Shortly after his return home, we watched his health rapidly decline. It surprised me he lived through the trial.

It's impossible to explain the demons and horrors that faced men returning from Vietnam. Many suffered drug dependency. For them there was a cure. For others, it was concern over exposure to Agent Orange, a deadly herbicide used to obliterate vegetation.

In the United States, farmers used the chemical extensively to control weeds, along with a pesticide to control insects. Used in Vietnam, the same herbicide had been concentrated to kill thick jungle vegetation.

Twenty-five years later, there are areas in Vietnam where Agent Orange penetrated the earth to such a depth that it is still sterile of any live vegetation.

For many men returning stateside, the contamination effects didn't suddenly appear. As in Mark's case, it was slow to develop. He suffered first from unconventional blood discrepancy symptoms. He developed leukemia and later, painful lesions spread throughout his body and painful tumors appeared along his spine leaving him in constant pain and a dependency on pain-killing drugs.

Letters from our official government documents admit, 'There has been no positive findings the United States Military use of Agent Orange is responsible for the sickness and early death of military men, but little research exists.'

The military isn't about to admit men were dying as a result of troops maneuvering through dense growth after planes had dumped thousands of gallons of concentrated Agent Orange on them and the surrounding vegetation. The chemicals saturated the soldiers' clothing and came in direct contact with their bodies.

The United States Military medical units treat the soldiers as the symptoms erupt but compensation due families of these men has never been agreed upon.

In fact, men discharged from the service and later showed signs of health problems while working in private sector positions, found their health providers refused to cover pre-existing conditions.

Soldiers who had served time in the service were eligible for medical treatment. Manifested symptoms were treated in military hospitals.

Luckily for Paula and Mark, they resided in Tacoma not far from Madigan military hospital. Other families were distance separated in order for the men to receive medical attention at a military medical facility in another part of the country.

"We wives," my sister told us, "write letters and visit our congressmen concerning the great hardship families endure when women must work outside the home to support the family and we haven't time to visit our loved ones, but they turn deaf ears to us."

Paula recently told me, some twenty-five years later, that she finally received a pittance check from the Dow Chemical Company, who were sued along with the United States Defense Department, for hardships created due to use of the chemicals.

"But, Jo," she told me, "my children are grown and at the time I needed financial assistance to cover the hardship created by Mark's condition, the government refused to acknowledge the problem was their responsibility."

Mr. Dennis, Mark's appointed attorney, spoke a language that left much to be desired by the tender ear. He was gruff, but I think it stemmed from his impatience with people like my sister, who are slow to be convinced that his knowledge of the legal system demanded respect.

At the time, my response to Paula, who didn't understand him or the law, which most common people don't, "We aren't familiar with how the legal system works, Paula, and, as you once told me, let Mr. Dennis do his job."

How well I remember the day of the trial. A beautiful day. We were still enjoying the warmth of summer—a day wasted if spent indoors.

Paula was finally convinced after Mark's doctor warned her that Mark had little time left ... a matter of days. "His organs responsible for bodily functions have begun to shut down and his mind won't be coherent much longer, plus drugs will only ease his pain for a limited time."

The day of the trial, the families of Mark and Paula who could attend came in support. Glen and I escorted Paula to the courthouse. We had just arrived when we noticed and heard a group of angry voices at the top of the stairs leading into the building.

The group broke apart when they noticed us. They abruptly turned and entered the building. It appeared to us an effort to evade meeting us face to face.

In the center of the group I recognized Kathy being carried swiftly along as they proceeded. She looked woebegone as if she had been crying.

"I recognize Kathy's parents," Paula whispered, "and the others must be family members." We watched them pass through the automatic doors to be swallowed up in the crowd massed in the lobby of the courthouse.

Glen's ability to handle a stressful time is a virtue. Once inside he noticed a vender in one corner and suggested coffee. "We have time before we have to appear in court."

Paula and I, in no mood for the invitation, refused the offer.

Our nerves were already taut as a violin string stretched to the snapping point but strained to endure a tweak more tension.

We experienced a confusing moment at the elevators—several on both sides of the lobby—as to which one the Bishops entered. After their verbal anger witnessed outside, we wished to avoid them.

In a judge-heard trial, all parties must attend. We nervously awaited Mark's appearance. Special arrangements had been made for him. He would be attended by a nurse responsible for the function of his medical equipment.

At times, he'd endure moments of fading away from us. Nothing but passage of time lets him gain control of his mentality. What if this is one of those days? How will it be possible for the judge to conduct the trial if Mark isn't lucid?

A judge trial is the only type witnesses are allowed in the courtroom. When the bailiff opened the courtroom doors, we were ushered down the aisle lined with wooden benches known as the spectator sections of the courtroom. The judge's podium was straight ahead with lawyer tables on either side of the room separating them from the public by a low wooden railing with a swinging gate.

Kathy Bishop sat at her counselor's table. Her family occupied the spectator section to the right behind the wooden railing.

We filed to the left behind Mr. Dennis. He turned briefly acknowledging us from his table, but continued to nervously twist back and forth from the courtroom door back to the youthful judge conversing with the bailiff.

A disturbance at the courtroom door announced Mark. He was so emaciated, I didn't recognize him. In green uniforms under white lab coats, a male hospital attendant and nurse pushed Mark's wheelchair down the aisle as Mr. Dennis hastened to open the gate for the trio.

Blonde hair fastened in a ponytail, a stethoscope dangling around her neck, the young nurse helped position the wheelchair to where the counselor indicated and checked on Mark's comfort. A chair was placed for her at Mark's side while the attendant was ushered to a seat just outside the gate.

I wondered if Mark was strong enough to turn his head to look back at Paula, but I surmised he was conserving what strength he had for the ordeal ahead. It worried me, seeing his condition. *Does he possess enough stamina to endure till the trial is over?*

Court commenced as I'd experienced before. The judge introduced himself as Judge Luke Eng then described the nature of a non-jury procedure. He stated to Mark, "Under the circumstances, you must be lucid enough to understand the proceedings and if questioned, you must speak clearly and loud enough to be heard. Can you do this?"

I held my breath waiting for Mark's answer. In fact, Mr. Dennis leaned forward to repeat Judge Eng's statement and question, but Mark's voice, though weak, was clear.

"Yes, Your Honor."

Judge Eng, after swearing Mark in, next requested from Mr. Dennis a transcript of Mark's medical records, a drug profile and recent urine test documentation. The nurse handed the bailiff the requested documents. The judge requested duplicate copies for Miss Spellman while he scanned the papers.

We watched Mark's nurse adjust his pillows to a more comfortable position.

During Judge Eng's inspection of Mark's papers, I glanced over to Paula sitting rigid and upright on the edge of her seat. She had unconsciously shredded a Kleenex into minuscule pieces that covered her skirt and littered the floor around her.

Judge Eng, satisfied with Mark's medical profile, invited the attorneys to deliver their opening arguments, even though there was no jury to convince.

Each lawyer spoke, then Judge Eng questioned both parties before announcing his decision. "I hereby find from lack of evidence, the defendant Mark Markham is not guilty."

The entire Bishop family, even before Judge Eng concluded his statement, came up off their benches in an uproar.

Judge Eng's gavel was heard above their protests. He impatiently waited for them to quiet down.

After the room silenced, Judge Eng explained his verdict. "This case lacks evidence of the alleged crime. Neither attorney has convinced me there was enough evidence to show cause. The young lady has not convinced me she has been attacked. And from the evidence brought before me, I find the defendant unable to commit such an act. Therefore, due to lack of evidence this court is not convinced. "I hereby find for the defendant. Mark Markham is not guilty of the alleged offense. Case dismissed."

The Bishops again stormed up and out of their seats. Mr. Bishop, shaking his fists, threatened Mark. "You've not heard the last of this, you ... you—"

Mrs. Bishop, close behind her husband agreed. Her mouth contorted in a sneer. "We'll appeal, we're gonna appeal. You won't get away with this, you evil, vile man."

Mr. Bishop, ushered along by the bailiff, continued to protest, "My little girl, my baby," and hurled obscenities towards the judge, who silently watched the Bishops depart the courtroom.

After things quieted down, we watched Paula and the nurse walk alongside a fatigued Mark hastily wheeled away by the attendant down to the elevator then into a waiting ambulance.

That day and hour was a victory for Mark's honor and for his family, but I somehow knew I was witnessing the grand finale for our Mark.

Glen offered to follow the ambulance back to the hospital for Paula's sake.

"As much as I want to be with him," Paula reasoned, "I know he's had a beastly day. He needs rest. I'll go back with you, pick up the kids and see him tonight. If I let down now, I'm gonna bawl and I won't be able to stop."

I remember little of the court procedure, little of the trip home, or even the rest of the day. Only that Mark was a very sick man, but his name had been cleared.

Kathy was out of our lives. She never once spoke up to admit her guilt. I wish I could be assured Mark's children never need to know of this episode in their daddy's life.

I suggested I keep Tammy and Jeff for a few days allowing Paula time to spend with Mark. Though it was never mentioned by any family member, we all knew she was about to lose her man, her soul mate, the father of her children.

Paula, to this day, blames herself for taking so long to decide on a judge or jury trial for Mark. He was never confronted with making the decision. She felt it best handled that way.

It was shortly after the trial that Mark lost his battle in his fight against Agent Orange exposure. He had faced two battles, and in the end, in a sense he won but one.

I remember I woke to the sound of a telephone. It was the middle of the night and instinctively I knew why it was ringing.

We hurried Tammy and Jeff back to Tacoma to be at their father's side. Glen and I held our tears; it wasn't our turn to grieve.

Paula requested a full military funeral for Mark, to honor her husband and for the benefit of his children.

During the ceremony, I looked up to see Mr. Dennis in attendance. He'd come to offer his respects to Paula and the children. I knew why I liked the man. He represented a friend. Afterwards, I cornered him to ask his opinion on the reason for having ordinary citizens sit on juries. Is this not a detriment to the law? Or is this a legal approach to keep in touch with common sense and our sense of justice?

His response: "Ordinary citizens? Who are ordinary citizens? How many so-called ordinary citizens vote? How many are Republicans or Democrats? How many take part in what they feel is political injustice? How about how many read a newspaper or watch news on TV? These are ordinary citizens. How do you figure their brand of common sense?

"As for me," I remember him saying, "I'd rather a judge settle my case—any day—I can tell you this."